Danger in the Fourth Dimension

As the ride barreled down a steep decline, Joe saw the man in the alien costume crawling over the back of a roller coaster car toward him. Just then Frank slid into Joe's car and said, "We've got company."

The masked alien lunged at Joe. One of the man's claws tightened around Joe's neck. Joe managed to choke out, "Frank . . . help!"

Frank hurled himself forward and pushed hard against the alien's chest. "Get off him!" Frank growled. The alien's grip on Joe loosened.

Suddenly the roller coaster entered a dark cavern. Joe felt a fist slam hard into his stomach. Breathless, he clutched his middle and sank to the seat of the car. Then he saw the alien elbow Frank in the stomach. "Hold on, Frank!" Joe cried out.

Frank staggered backward. He'd lost his balance and was about to fall off the speeding roller coaster!

The Hardy Boys Mystery Stories

#59	Night of the Werewolf	#90	Danger on the Diamond
#60	Mystery of the Samurai Sword	#91	Shield of Fear
		#92	The Shadow Killers
#61	The Pentagon Spy	#93	The Serpent's Tooth Mystery
#62	The Apeman's Secret	#94	Breakdown in Axeblade
#63	The Mummy Case	#95	Danger on the Air
#64	Mystery of Smugglers Cove	#96	Wipeout
#65	The Stone Idol	#97	Cast of Criminals
#66	The Vanishing Thieves	#98	Spark of Suspicion
#67	The Outlaw's Silver	#99	Dungeon of Doom
#68	Deadly Chase	#100	The Secret of the Island Treasure
#69	The Four-headed Dragon		
#70	The Infinity Clue	#101	The Money Hunt
#71	Track of the Zombie	#102	Terminal Shock
#72	The Voodoo Plot	#103	The Million-Dollar Nightmare
#73	The Billion Dollar Ransom		
#74	Tic-Tac-Terror	#104	Tricks of the Trade
#75	Trapped at Sea	#105	The Smoke Screen Mystery
#76	Game Plan for Disaster	#106	Attack of the Video Villains
#77	The Crimson Flame	#107	Panic on Gull Island
#78	Cave-in!	#108	Fear on Wheels
#79	Sky Sabotage	#109	The Prime-Time Crime
#80	The Roaring River Mystery	#110	The Secret of Sigma Seven
#81	The Demon's Den	#111	Three-Ring Terror
#82	The Blackwing Puzzle	#112	The Demolition Mission
#83	The Swamp Monster	#113	Radical Moves
#84	Revenge of the Desert Phantom	#114	The Case of the Counterfeit Criminals
#85	The Skyfire Puzzle		
#86	The Mystery of the Silver Star	#115	Sabotage at Sports City
		#116	Rock 'n' Roll Renegades
#87	Program for Destruction	#117	The Baseball Card Conspiracy
#88	Tricky Business		
#89	The Sky Blue Frame	#118	Danger in the Fourth Dimension

Available from MINSTREL Books

118

The HARDY BOYS®

DANGER IN THE FOURTH DIMENSION

FRANKLIN W. DIXON

A MINSTREL® BOOK

PUBLISHED BY POCKET BOOKS

New York   London   Toronto   Sydney   Tokyo   Singapore

This book is a work of fiction. Names, characters, places, and incidents are either the product of the author's imagination or are used fictitiously. Any resemblance to actual events or locales or persons, living or dead, is entirely coincidental.

A MINSTREL PAPERBACK *ORIGINAL*

 A Minstrel Book published by
POCKET BOOKS, a division of Simon & Schuster Inc.
1230 Avenue of the Americas, New York, NY 10020

Copyright © 1993 by Simon & Schuster Inc.

Front cover illustration by Daniel Horne

Produced by Mega-Books of New York, Inc.

ISBN: 0-671-79308-X

First Minstrel Books printing February 1993

10 9 8 7 6 5 4 3 2 1

THE HARDY BOYS MYSTERY STORIES is a trademark of Simon & Schuster Inc.

THE HARDY BOYS, A MINSTREL BOOK, and colophon are registered trademarks of Simon & Schuster Inc.

Printed in the U.S.A.

Contents

1. Welcome to the Fourth Dimension   1
2. A Sudden Exit   10
3. Clues to a Crime   21
4. Beware Falling Objects   30
5. A Deadly Game   39
6. Followed   51
7. A Near Miss   60
8. Up in Smoke   70
9. Virtual Reality   77
10. A Rough Flight   85
11. The Masked Alien   95
12. Caught in the Act   105
13. A Dirty Trick   116
14. Scam Time   126
15. Escape to a New Dimension   139
16. War of the Worlds   147

DANGER IN THE
FOURTH DIMENSION

1 Welcome to the Fourth Dimension

"What would you say if I told you we were going to spend our spring vacation in another dimension?" Frank Hardy asked his brother, Joe.

Joe had just stepped into the Hardys' house, a basketball under his arm. "What are you talking about?" the muscular seventeen-year-old said. "Some kind of a sci-fi movie?"

Frank laughed. At six foot one, eighteen-year-old Frank was an inch taller and slightly thinner than his brother, and had dark hair and brown eyes. "Actually, I was talking about the Fourth Dimension. It's that theme park in South Carolina that features futuristic high-tech and sci-fi exhibits and rides, remember?"

Joe pushed his blond hair off his forehead. "Yeah.

1

The staff there dresses up like aliens. It's like time traveling to another universe."

Frank went on. "Dad called just before you got home. He's investigating a case at the Fourth Dimension and needs our help. How about driving down there tonight? Dad's reserved a room for us at the Galaxy Hotel in the park."

Frank and Joe's father, Fenton Hardy, was a retired New York City police officer who had become a private detective.

"Sure," Joe said. "What's the case?"

"Dad didn't say," Frank replied. "He just told me he'd fill us in at breakfast. We're supposed to meet him in his room at eight tomorrow morning."

Frank glanced at his watch. "We'd better get moving. It's almost two o'clock, and it's going to take us at least ten hours to drive down there."

Joe nodded. "Just give me fifteen minutes to shower, change, and pack," he said as he put the basketball away in the hall closet.

"This is great," Joe said to his brother as they headed upstairs. "Not only do we get to solve a case on our vacation, but we also get to hang out at one of the best parks in the States. The Fourth Dimension has the fastest, steepest roller coaster ever designed. I can't wait to check it out."

It was after midnight when Frank turned onto the road leading to the Fourth Dimension theme park. There were no other cars on the two-lane road, and the only light came from the high beams of the Hardys' dark blue van.

Frank opened the window and breathed in the cool, fresh, pine-scented air. He was looking forward to this vacation. In Bayport it had been cold and snowy, but down in South Carolina spring had definitely arrived.

Suddenly Frank glimpsed a tall structure rising from the landscape about three miles ahead. As he drove closer, he saw that it was a clock tower with a glowing red dial. A spaceship in the center of the dial pointed at twinkling white stars that indicated the numbers. The clock said it was twenty after twelve. Below the clock was a white neon sign that said The Fourth Dimension.

Frank nudged his brother. "Wake up, Joe."

Joe opened his eyes, then sat up straight and stretched. "Is it my turn to drive?" he asked sleepily.

"Not worth it," Frank replied, pointing at the clock tower. "See? We're almost there."

The road began to slope uphill. When the Hardys got to the top of the rise, Frank stopped the van to look at the Fourth Dimension complex spread out before them. The approach to the park was lit by street lamps, and Frank and Joe could see the peaks, loops, and tunnels of the roller coaster ride that curved in a semicircle around the perimeter of the park. Inside the semicircle were buildings of all shapes and sizes, including a pyramid and a geodes-

3

ic dome. A monorail circled the park and connected each building.

"Awesome," Frank said quietly. "It's like a whole futuristic city."

"Let's find our futuristic hotel, okay?" Joe said with a yawn. "I'll appreciate the Fourth Dimension better after a good night's sleep."

Frank continued down the road. Several moments later, he saw the entrance to the park straight ahead and the visitors' parking lot off to the left, just outside the park. To the right was a sign marked Galaxy Hotel. Frank drove toward the fifteen-story building, which was a hexagon shape, and pulled into the parking lot.

Frank and Joe entered the hotel and headed across the quiet, dimly lit lobby to the reception desk. Both Hardys were impressed by a painting of the Milky Way that stretched the length of the domed ceiling.

Suddenly, they saw a tall figure with one huge eye and an enormous mouth with sharp fangs rise up from behind the desk. The creature was dressed in scaly armor. It stretched out its arms and said in a deep voice, "Greetings, visitors. Welcome to the Fourth Dimension."

Joe stared at the creature's clawlike hands. Then he turned to his brother and said, "Uh, Frank, are we still on the planet earth?"

The creature behind the desk laughed. Then it grabbed a flap of skin under its chin and pulled upward. The horrible face disappeared, and the

4

Hardys saw the smiling face of a very normal-looking man emerge. He had sandy-colored hair and brown eyes. He glanced briefly at his black digital watch. Frank noticed that it was a lot like the one that he himself was wearing. Strange choice for an alien, Frank thought.

"I guess it's a little late to expect new guests to get into the spirit of the Fourth Dimension," the man said. He stripped off his rubber claws and held out one hand. "I'm Mike Strauss, the manager of the Galaxy Hotel."

"I'm Frank Hardy, and this is my brother, Joe," Frank said, shaking hands. "I think you have a reservation for us. Our dad, Fenton Hardy, requested a room next to his."

The manager turned to the computer and began typing in some commands. "Right," he said after a few moments. "You're staying here for a week. Room 902." He reached up and took a large white envelope off the shelf above the computer.

"This packet contains your room keys, maps of the park, and a schedule of events," Strauss explained, handing the envelope to Frank. "There's a video inside that will give you a good idea of the Fourth Dimension's attractions. If you need anything, I'm on duty here most days. I hope you enjoy your stay."

The Hardys thanked him and headed for the elevator. While they were waiting for it to arrive, Frank looked around the lobby. When his glance fell on Mike Strauss, he saw the hotel manager look at his watch again, then disappear into a small office behind the desk.

He's probably going back there to take a nap, Frank thought. He yawned. He could use some sleep himself. It had been a long day.

When the Hardys got to their room on the ninth floor, Joe unpacked, then took the video tape out of the envelope and popped it into the VCR under the TV.

"What are you doing?" Frank asked as he climbed into his bed. "Don't you want to get some sleep?"

"I'm not tired right now," Joe replied, his eyes on the TV and one hand on the remote control on the night table between the beds. "I really want to take a look at this video. I'll keep the sound low, okay?"

He glanced over at his brother and saw that Frank was already dozing off. Joe lay back and watched as a camera panned over the theme park.

Despite what he had just said to Frank, Joe began to feel drowsy. He pressed the VCR Stop button on the remote control, closed his eyes, and drifted off to sleep.

A muffled cry woke Joe up. He heard a thudding sound, as if someone had fallen to the floor. Then silence. Finally, Joe realized that he had forgotten to turn off the TV when he turned off the VCR. The network was showing a robbery scene from an episode of an old black-and-white detective series.

That TV show must have been what I heard, Joe thought as he pressed the button to turn it off. He glanced at the clock next to the remote. It said two-fifteen. He fell back against the pillows, and a few moments later, he was asleep.

When Joe opened his eyes at seven-thirty the next morning, he saw Frank standing by the window. His brother was already dressed.

"So what kind of view do we have?" Joe asked.

Frank shrugged. "Not a very good one. This side of the hotel doesn't face the park. All I can see is part of the roller coaster ride and a construction site about a quarter of a mile away."

Joe got out of bed and padded across the room. "We won't be spending much time in here, anyway," he said as he pulled some clothes out of his suitcase. "If I know Dad, he'll have us running around the entire park searching for clues."

After Joe had finished dressing, the brothers stepped next door to their father's room. Frank knocked on the door. When there was no answer, he knocked again. "Dad?" he called. Again there was no answer.

Joe tried the door. It was locked. "He's probably in the restaurant eating breakfast," Joe said. "I could definitely use some breakfast, too."

Frank nodded. "Same here."

But when the brothers entered the restaurant—a large room on the third floor that overlooked the park—there was no sign of Fenton Hardy.

A hostess in a silver-colored jumpsuit covered with stars led Frank and Joe to a table.

7

"I bet Dad's out in the park somewhere following a lead," Joe said as they settled into their chairs. "You know what his motto is: 'Work first, eat later.'"

"That's true," Frank said with a laugh. He looked down at his menu. "We'd better order now, before he shows up and decides *we* should work first and eat later."

After they had ordered, the brothers sat back and glanced around the room at the guests. There were several families, a large number of older couples, and single men and women who looked to be in their fifties and sixties. Some of the older couples had grandchildren with them.

An elderly couple at the table behind Frank stood up and started to leave the restaurant. Joe noticed that they had left a brochure behind on the table. He got up, grabbed the brochure, and hurried after the couple. He glanced at the brochure, which advertised New Dimension Retirement Village—A New Concept in Leisure Living.

Joe caught up to the couple, who thanked him for returning the brochure. When he got back to his table, his brother had already started on his breakfast.

"It's eight-thirty now," Frank said as Joe reached for a slice of French toast. "Maybe Dad went back to his room. I'd better go up and see if he's waiting for us there."

Joe nodded. "I'll stick around in case he shows up here."

Frank took a last bite of French toast and drained his glass of orange juice. Then he pushed back his chair, stood up, and left the restaurant.

Several minutes later, he was knocking on the door of his father's room again. This time, the door opened, and Frank found himself facing a chambermaid with long, flowing blond hair and thick glasses. She was dressed in fluorescent green overalls and a yellow turtleneck shirt. Frank saw that her name tag said Meg—Housekeeping.

"Excuse me," Frank said. "I'm looking for Fenton Hardy. But I guess he's not here if you're cleaning his room."

The young woman frowned. "Mr. Hardy's not staying at this hotel anymore," she said. "He's checked out."

2 A Sudden Exit

Frank stared at the chambermaid. "That's impossible," he insisted. "Our dad couldn't have checked out. I *know* he's staying here."

The young woman shrugged. "Well, I was told to make up this room for a new guest," she said. "See?" She opened the door a little wider so that Frank could see the stripped bed. A laundry duffel bag and a black garbage bag sat on the floor.

"And now, if you don't mind," the chambermaid continued, "I'd like to get back to work. I've got lots of rooms to clean." She shut the door firmly.

Frank stood in the hallway a moment, baffled. Then he headed back down to the restaurant.

"Checked out?" Joe exclaimed after Frank told him what the chambermaid had said. "But that

doesn't make any sense. Why would Dad just decide to leave?"

"Good question," Frank replied. "And here's another one. If he *did* check out, why didn't he let us know?"

"Maybe he left word for us at the front desk," Joe suggested. He placed his napkin on the table and stood up. "Let's go talk to Mike Strauss. Dad probably left a message with him."

When the Hardys entered the lobby, they spotted the hotel manager standing behind the desk. He was talking to a short, balding man in a tweed jacket and bow tie who appeared to be in his fifties. Frank saw that Strauss was still dressed in the alien costume he had been wearing the night before, but wasn't wearing his mask.

"Excuse me," Frank said as he and Joe approached the desk. "I'm sorry to interrupt, Mr. Strauss, but when you're free, could we speak to you for a moment?"

The manager turned toward them. His face seemed very pale, and there were dark circles under his eyes. "I'm free now," he said with a weak smile. "What can I do for you?"

"We were told that our father, Fenton Hardy, checked out last night," Frank said. "Is that true?"

Strauss put his hand to his forehead and groaned.

"Uh, are you feeling okay?" Joe asked the manager.

"No, not really," Strauss replied. "My head is aching, and I feel kind of dizzy."

11

The short, balding man took Strauss by the arm. "I think you'd better sit down, Mike," he said firmly. He led the manager over to an armchair.

Joe shot a questioning look at his brother, but Frank just shrugged. He and Joe followed the two men and sat down on the sofa opposite the armchair.

Mike Strauss closed his eyes and took a deep breath. "Thank you, Justin," he said to the short man. "I think I'm feeling a little better now." The manager looked at Frank and Joe. "I'm sorry, what were you saying? Oh, yes, you were asking about your father. Well, he definitely did check out."

"Did he leave a note for us on his way out?" Joe asked.

Strauss hesitated for a moment. Then he said slowly, "There wasn't a note. And, well, to tell you the truth, I didn't actually *see* Fenton Hardy leave the hotel. He used the electronic checkout on his TV to indicate that he was leaving today. TV checkout is an option we offer our guests," the manager added.

"But he still would have had to stop by the desk to settle his bill, or at least pass by on his way out," Frank pressed. "Didn't you see him then?"

Strauss shook his head. "I didn't see your father," he said, "because just before two A.M., while I was dozing at my desk in the office, someone grabbed me from behind and shoved a washcloth full of chloroform in my face. It must have been a

12

pretty hefty dose, because I'm still feeling the effects of it."

Frank and Joe exchanged confused glances.

"When I came to at about seven A.M.," Strauss continued, "I saw that the door to the office safe was open and some money had been stolen. The key to the safe was still inside the lock."

"Have you contacted the police?" Joe asked.

"Not yet," Strauss replied.

"First Andrew Taylor, the owner of the Fourth Dimension, has to be notified about the theft," the bald man broke in. "I'm sure he'll insist on total discretion from the police. The park doesn't need a lot of bad publicity."

"You can count on us to keep quiet about the theft," Frank said quickly.

Strauss nodded and stood up. "I guess I'd better call Taylor right now," he said with a sigh. "I just hope he doesn't lose his temper and fire me for negligence. I can't afford to lose this job." He hurried off in the direction of his office.

The short man watched Strauss enter his office. Then he sat down in the chair vacated by the manager and looked intently at Frank and Joe.

"My name is Justin Maceda, and I work here at the Fourth Dimension," he said in a low tone. "I need to speak with you about your father."

Joe sat up straight and leaned toward Maceda. "Have you seen Dad?" he asked eagerly.

"No, I haven't," Maceda replied.

13

The Hardys saw Maceda look past them toward the hotel entrance, an agitated expression on his face. Frank and Joe turned and saw a tall, silver-haired man in a three-piece suit striding across the lobby.

"We can't talk here," Maceda said quickly. "We need privacy. I suggest we continue this conversation in your room." He stood up and started for the elevator.

Totally puzzled, Frank and Joe followed him. When they entered the Hardys' room, Maceda shut the door and turned to face Frank and Joe.

"That silver-haired man you saw in the lobby was Andrew Taylor, the owner I mentioned earlier," he explained. "I couldn't take the chance that he might overhear us. You see, the safe robbery was the third theft to take place here at the park. A computer was stolen from the park's Command Center a few weeks ago. And I was the victim of the second theft. I don't want Andrew to know that."

"But he's your boss," Frank said. "Shouldn't he be told, especially now that there have been three crimes?"

"What does all this have to do with our father, anyway?" Joe asked impatiently.

With a loud sigh, Maceda sat down on the edge of a bed. Then he looked up at Frank and Joe. "I was getting to that. I hired your father to investigate the theft of two blueprint designs from my office. I'm an architect," he explained. "I designed the Fourth

14

Dimension, including the rides, exhibits, and the computer network that controls the whole operation. The stolen blueprints were my exclusive design for two new attractions here at the park."

"But I still don't see why you never reported the theft of the blueprints to Andrew Taylor," Frank said.

Maceda sighed again and looked down at the floor. "Andrew is an extremely demanding man. He's also extremely short-tempered." Maceda looked up at the Hardys with a worried expression. "He's been expecting those attractions to be ready for months. I knew he'd have a fit if I told him the blueprints were stolen. He'd probably even accuse me of lying about the theft to gain more time."

"So you were hoping Dad would catch the thief and recover the designs," Joe said. "And Taylor would never have to know anything about the whole incident."

"That's it exactly," Maceda replied. "So you can see why I'm unhappy to hear that Fenton Hardy has checked out of the Galaxy."

"It's not like Dad to walk out on a case," Frank said. "He must have had a good reason for leaving the hotel."

"That's right," Joe agreed. "My guess is he's still around here somewhere, secretly following up a lead. We're supposed to be helping him with this case, so it's just a matter of time before he contacts us."

"And when he does, we'll let you know, Mr. Maceda," Frank reassured him.

Maceda stood up and smiled for the first time. "Thank you," he said, sounding relieved. "You've both been very helpful. You can reach me anytime at the park's Command Center, right next to the Space Flight Building. I'm usually in by seven-thirty A.M. And now, if you'll excuse me, I really must get to work."

After Maceda had left, Frank went over to the night table and pulled a telephone book out of the drawer. He sat down on the bed and began to leaf through it.

"I get the feeling you're not satisfied with the explanation we just gave Maceda about why Dad checked out," Joe said.

Frank stopped turning the pages and looked over at his brother. "Look, Joe, it doesn't make sense. Dad wouldn't leave us hanging like this. If everything was okay, he would have gotten in touch with us by now."

"So who are you calling?" Joe asked.

"I'm going to try the airport and then the car rental agencies," Frank replied. "He must have flown or driven a rental car out of this area."

"I'll use the pay phone in the lobby to call Mom and Aunt Gertrude," Joe said, heading for the door. "Maybe they've heard from him."

Frank nodded. "Call Con Riley, too," he called after his brother. "Maybe Dad contacted him."

16

Lieutenant Con Riley of the Bayport police was a friend of the Hardys and often helped them with their cases.

An hour later, Joe returned to the room to find his brother still sitting on the bed, the phone book in his lap. He was staring at the telephone.

Frank looked up at his brother. "Has anyone heard from him?" he asked hopefully.

Joe shook his head. "Did you find out anything?" he asked.

"Only that Dad didn't book a flight out of the area and didn't rent a car from any of the local agencies," Frank replied. "I even called the taxi companies to see if anyone named Fenton Hardy had requested a pickup from the Fourth Dimension. No luck there, either."

"This is crazy." Joe said, his voice rising with frustration. "Where *is* he?"

Just then, there was a knock at the door.

The brothers looked at each other, their eyes wide. They were both thinking the same thing: Maybe it's Dad!

But when Joe opened the door, he saw a brown-haired chambermaid with an armload of fresh towels smiling at him.

"Hi," she said brightly. "I'm Denise. Can I make up your room now?"

"Uh, sure," Joe replied, opening the door wider. "We'll leave so we won't be in your way."

Suddenly Joe had an idea. "Excuse me, Denise,"

17

he said, "but we just got a call from our father. He was staying in the room next door until today, and he told us he left his shaving kit behind." Joe flashed her his most charming smile. "Could you let us into the room so we can get it?"

The young woman smiled back at him. "No problem," she said. "Guests leave stuff in their rooms all the time. I'll be happy to let you in."

"Nice work," Frank whispered to his brother as they followed the chambermaid out the door. "Now we can search Dad's room for clues."

Joe nodded. "That was the idea, big brother."

As soon as they were inside Room 904, Joe shut the door gently. Then the brothers got to work.

Frank looked through the dresser while Joe searched the bathroom. Then they checked the closet and the night table drawers.

"Not a single clue," Joe said, disappointed. "There's nothing here."

"Keep looking," Frank said as he knelt down in front of the armchair. "Sometimes clues are easy to overlook." He thrust his hand between the cushions of the chair. Suddenly he felt a small piece of paper. He pulled it out and stared at it.

"What is it?" Joe asked, joining his brother by the armchair.

"It's a scrap of notepaper," Frank told him. "Someone scribbled the words 'New Dimension Retirement Village and Doherty-Howell Development Company' on it." He handed the piece of paper to his brother.

"The brochure I returned to that couple in the restaurant was for the same retirement village," Joe observed. He turned the piece of paper over. "That's strange. Someone wrote down a phone number on the back—with the Bayport area code."

Frank stood up and turned to face his brother. "Better keep searching, Joe. That chambermaid's going to start wondering why it's taking us so long to find a shaving kit."

Joe thrust the piece of paper in his pocket and knelt down to look under the bed. He glimpsed a white washcloth on the floor about a foot away and reached under the bed to pull it out. The cloth felt damp.

As Joe got to his feet, he lifted the cloth to his nose and sniffed. All at once, the room began to spin. He dropped the washcloth and fell to his knees, grabbing onto the bed to steady himself.

"Joe, what is it? What's wrong?" Frank exclaimed, rushing over to his brother. He saw the cloth and picked it up.

"Don't sniff it," Joe gasped. "It's been soaked with chloroform." He pulled himself off the floor and sat down heavily on the bed. After he had taken a couple of deep breaths, he began to feel better.

As he watched Frank examine the washcloth, he remembered the muffled cry and thud he'd heard

19

in the middle of the night. With a growing sense of dread, he told his brother about it. "It wasn't the TV, Frank," he finished, his voice shaking.

"I guess not," Frank said grimly. "What you heard was our father being chloroformed—and kidnapped."

3 Clues to a Crime

"It was all my fault," Joe burst out. "I could have stopped them from kidnapping Dad!"

"Come on, Joe," Frank said quietly. "You can't blame yourself. You couldn't have known what was happening."

Joe shook his head in frustration. "I *should* have known," he muttered. "I'm supposed to be a detective."

"Dad's a detective, too—one of the best," Frank pointed out. "That didn't stop him from getting himself kidnapped. There's always an unknown risk factor in detective work—you know that."

After a moment, Joe nodded and managed half a smile. "That's true. I mean, think of all the risks we've taken during our cases. Anyway," he added,

21

getting to his feet, "the reality is that Dad's been kidnapped and we have to find him—fast. So, what's our first move?"

Before Frank could reply, the door opened and Denise, the maid, asked, "Did you find your father's shaving kit? Because I have to make up this room now."

"We were just leaving," Joe told her as he and Frank started for the door. "We, uh, couldn't find the kit. I guess our father made a mistake."

"I don't think you have to worry about this room," Frank said to Denise. "There was a chambermaid cleaning in here earlier. Her name was Meg."

"She's not supposed to do that," Denise said, frowning. "Mr. Strauss is very organized about which rooms we're supposed to clean. Unless he's changed the assignments. I'd better go find out." She turned and left the room before the brothers could say another word.

When the Hardys got back to their own room, Frank sat down in the armchair and said, "The first question we need to ask ourselves is why Dad was kidnapped."

Joe pulled out the desk chair and straddled it so that he faced Frank. "Well, he was investigating the theft of Justin Maceda's blueprints. Maybe the thief found out about Dad and wanted to get him out of the way so he could pull off more robberies at the park."

Frank nodded thoughtfully. "That makes sense.

22

It's also a strong possibility that the kidnapper is the same person who knocked out Mike Strauss and robbed the safe in his office. The attack on Strauss and the theft happened just before two A.M. The kidnapping took place soon after that. And both victims were chloroformed."

Joe pulled the scrap of paper out of his pocket and held it up. "What about this?" he asked. "Do you think it has anything to do with the kidnapping?"

"I'm not sure if there's a connection," Frank replied. "We don't even know if it belonged to Dad. It could have been left behind by someone who was staying in the room before him."

Joe looked at the telephone number on the back of the piece of paper. "The fact that this is a Bayport number makes me think it did belong to Dad. Maybe the phone number is connected to the case."

"Well, there's only one way to find out," Frank said. He got up from the chair, took the paper from Joe, and walked over to the phone. He dialed the number and waited for what seemed like a very long time.

Finally he heard a man's voice say that he couldn't come to the phone.

"Answering machine," Frank mouthed to Joe. Then he listened as the voice at the other end suggested he leave his name, phone number, and a brief message after the beep.

After Frank heard the beep, he said into the

23

phone, "This is Frank Hardy. I'm calling about my father, Fenton Hardy. I can be reached at the Fourth Dimension theme park." He gave the park's phone number and their room number before hanging up.

"The guy didn't give his name," Frank reported to his brother. "It looks like a dead end, but you never know."

Joe nodded. "What's next?" he asked.

"I think we should talk to the park security people," Frank replied. "We need to find out if Dad's being held somewhere in or outside the park. Security will be able to tell us if anyone left the park last night after two-fifteen—the time of the kidnapping."

Joe picked up the large white envelope Strauss had given them, pulled out the map of the theme park, and unfolded it. Frank looked at the map over his brother's shoulder. "Here's the security and first-aid center," Joe said, pointing to a building on the map. "We'll have to take the monorail to get to it. There's a stop right outside the hotel. Let's go."

He folded up the map and put it in his pocket. Then he and Frank left their room and headed for the elevator.

When Frank and Joe stepped out of the hotel, they spotted the monorail station off to their left. The entrance was a clear glass tube that sloped gently upward. A moving, carpeted floor took the Hardys and some parents with excited kids up to the station platform.

24

Frank and Joe looked around. They saw that the station was decorated with posters advertising the Fourth Dimension's exhibits and rides. Beyond the tracks, the Hardys could see visitors strolling through the park, waiting in lines, walking in and out of buildings, or resting on benches.

"Here it comes," Frank said. He nudged his brother, who had been gazing across the park at the roller coaster. It climbed slowly upward for fifty feet, then shot downward, disappearing into a tunnel.

Joe turned and saw the long, sleek, ten-car monorail train soundlessly approaching the station from the right. When the train stopped, its doors slid open with a hissing sound. The Hardys stepped into one of the middle cars and sat down. The door closed, and the boys heard a soft whirring sound as the monorail started to circle the park.

"The first stop is the Sight and Sound movie theater," Joe said, glancing at the map and then out the window at a round, black and white building. "Next is the Biosphere, whatever that is."

"It's an experimental structure that tries to re-create the earth's land, water, and air," Frank explained. "But it's done on a smaller scale, of course. Re-creating a biosphere will be important if people ever try to colonize space."

"That would make a good theme park attraction someday—a ride up to a space colony," Joe said with a grin as they passed the white, windowless Biosphere.

After the train had stopped at the Home of the Future and the Video Arcade, Joe consulted the map and said, "I think we should get off at the next stop, the Hall of Holograms. That's the closest station to the security center."

A few moments later, the monorail stopped at the Hall of Holograms. The brothers stepped out of the train onto the platform and saw that the station was enclosed by a dome and decorated with TV screens displaying various hologram images. A short walkway connected the station to the pyramid-shaped building that housed the hologram exhibit.

Frank and Joe found another clear glass tube marked Exit to Park. After they had ridden the moving floor down to street level, they headed toward the security center. As they walked, they noticed several park employees answering visitors' questions and giving directions. Most wore shiny silver- or gold-colored jumpsuits, but some were dressed up to look like aliens. A few wore the same scaly armor, mask, and rubber claws Mike Strauss had been wearing. Every staff member the Hardys saw wore a black metallic badge printed with a name and employee ID number.

When Frank and Joe entered the white brick security and first-aid center, they approached a uniformed security officer behind a desk who was using a computer.

"Excuse me," Frank said to her.

The young woman looked up at the Hardys. "Yes?" she said with a smile. "Can I help you?"

"We're here on vacation," Frank explained, "but we're also doing an article for our school newspaper on the Fourth Dimension and how it operates on a day-to-day basis."

Frank glanced at his brother. Joe nodded slightly. He understood that Frank didn't want to reveal their father's situation. Getting the park authorities involved in the kidnapping at this point might jeopardize Fenton Hardy's safety.

"And you want to interview the security staff, right?" the woman said. "Well, I just started working here, but I'll be happy to answer your questions if I can."

"Could you tell us if there's a security guard stationed at the park entrance all night?" Frank asked. "And if there's a guard at the service entrance of the hotel?"

"Yes to both questions," the woman replied. "From what I've heard, our boss, Mr. Taylor, isn't exactly the trusting type. In fact, security guards have to search every delivery *and* employee vehicle that leaves the Fourth Dimension, day or night, to see if anything's been stolen from the park. It seems kind of crazy to me that an amusement park would need such tight security," she added with a shrug. "But this is my first job, and I guess I have a lot to learn."

"Well, I think we have enough material for our article," Frank told her. "Thanks for your help."

"My pleasure," the young woman said, smiling.

The Hardys left the building and began walking

northeast through the park in the direction of the Space Flight Building.

"Taylor must have ordered the vehicles searched because of the computer theft," Joe said. "With all that extra security, I don't see how the kidnapper could have smuggled Dad out of here. He's got to be somewhere in the park. All we have to do is turn the place upside down."

"It won't be easy," Frank pointed out. "Security is tight, and there are a lot of guards and staff people around. We need to find a way to investigate these buildings without arousing suspicion."

"I've got it," Joe said, snapping his fingers. "Why don't we see if Justin Maceda can get us jobs at the park. As staff members we'll be able to move freely inside any building."

"My brother the genius," Frank said. "Let's head over to the Command Center now and talk to Maceda."

When they reached the monorail station next to the Space Flight Building, the Hardys stopped for a moment to admire the large models of the sun, planets, and stars of the Milky Way that stood on pedestals along the length of the platform. The large globes were molded with different colored metals—gold, silver, brass, and copper. A crowd of people was standing on the platform, waiting for the monorail to approach the station. There were a few staffers among the crowd, including a maintenance worker wearing a gray jumpsuit, sunglasses, and a cap. He was carrying a small toolbox and a ladder.

Joe stepped back to get a better view of the earth model, which stood atop a ten-foot stand. The planet was about four feet in diameter, with the continents and oceans sized to scale.

"Let me see the map," Frank said.

Joe handed it to him, then glanced up at the models again. Suddenly, he saw the globe of the earth begin to shake with the vibrations of the oncoming monorail. The crowd surged as people began to move toward the train. The model wobbled, then toppled over, falling straight toward Frank!

4 Beware Falling
Objects

"Frank! Look out!" Joe shouted. He hurled himself at his brother, pushing Frank onto the sidewalk. A split second later the falling sphere crashed to the ground—right where Frank had been standing just seconds earlier.

The people in the area gasped. A staff member dressed up as Loid, the green-skinned android from the sci-fi movie *Annihilator,* rushed over to the Hardys. "Are you okay?" he asked Frank.

"Yeah," Frank gasped. "I'm always up for a spontaneous football scrimmage." Joe's tackle had knocked the wind out of Frank, but after taking a few deep breaths, he was able to breathe normally. "What happened?" he asked as he got to his feet.

"The earth model almost fell on top of you," Joe said, pointing at the model on the sidewalk.

"I'd better notify maintenance right away," said Loid, the staffer. "There may be another loose model up there." He hurried off.

The brothers stepped over to the model and crouched down next to it. "Here's the mount that attaches the model to the column," Frank said. "Look at this—the bolts that hold the mount in place are missing." He looked at his brother. "I think someone deliberately took out those bolts and pushed the model off the stand. And I wouldn't be surprised if it was the same guy who kidnapped Dad."

"Wait a minute," Joe said as he and Frank straightened up. "There was a maintenance man on the platform carrying a toolbox and a ladder. Maybe he was pretending to fix the model, but he really went up there to remove the bolts. Maybe he gave the pedestal a push while everyone was paying attention to the arriving train. But if the person who did this was the kidnapper, what's his motive for trying to deck you?"

"Maybe he found out we're Fenton Hardy's sons, and he figured we'd come looking for Dad," Frank said. "The question is, how did he figure out who we are?"

The brothers walked toward the Command Center, lost in thought, ignoring the noisy laughter and chatter of the people they passed.

Suddenly Joe stopped short. "I just realized something," he said. "The only person who knows that Fenton Hardy is our father is Mike Strauss. What if he made up the story about being chloroformed? He could have kidnapped Dad first, then robbed the safe. He'd feel more secure about pulling off another theft once he got Dad out of the way. And it would have been really easy for him to make it look like Dad checked out of the hotel."

"It's a possibility," Frank agreed. "But if Strauss is the kidnapper *and* the thief, how did he find out that Dad was investigating for Maceda and that we're detectives?"

"Maybe Dad told Maceda about us," Joe suggested. "And Maceda confided in Strauss. They seem to be good friends. When we see Maceda, we can ask him about Strauss." He pointed straight ahead at a small copper-colored building shaped like a flying saucer. "That's the Command Center," he said.

When Frank and Joe entered the building, they saw that it was one big room with three offices at the back. Staff people dressed in red and black uniforms sat at computer work stations throughout the room.

The middle office was Justin Maceda's. The door was open, and the Hardys could see the architect behind his desk working at his computer. He had changed into the same uniform worn by the other staff members in the Command Center.

Maceda got up and pulled a book from a shelf on the back wall of the office. His eyes lit up when he saw the Hardys standing in the doorway. "Ah! Frank and Joe," he said with a smile. "Come in and shut the door." He motioned to two chairs in front of his desk. "Sit down. Have you heard any word from your father?"

"Actually, we . . ." Frank began. But before he could say anything else, a connecting door to the next office opened and a slim young woman with short brown hair wearing the Command Center uniform burst into Maceda's office. Joe noticed a small, strawberry-colored birthmark on her neck.

"Justin, I—" the young woman started to say. Then she saw the Hardys. "Oh," she said in confusion. "I'm sorry, Justin. I didn't realize you were busy."

"It's quite all right, Laurel," Maceda said warmly. He turned to the Hardys. "Frank and Joe, I'd like to introduce Laurel Kramer. Laurel is my assistant. I simply couldn't run the Fourth Dimension without her."

Laurel rolled her eyes. "That's a total exaggeration, Justin, and you know it," she said with a laugh. "But thanks for the compliment."

"My pleasure. You look like you have important news for me," Maceda guessed.

"It's just that I was testing the Space Shuttle Simulator and it malfunctioned," Laurel replied quickly. "We can talk about it when you're free."

33

She smiled at the Hardys. "Nice to have met you." Then she turned and disappeared back into her office.

"That young woman left a promising career designing special effects for the film industry to come and work with me," Maceda told Frank and Joe. "She's an invaluable assistant and extremely ambitious. I'm sure it won't be long before she owns her own design company. But I didn't mean to change the subject," he added. "Have you heard from your father?"

"I'm afraid we have some bad news, Mr. Maceda," Frank said. "We've discovered that Dad has been kidnapped."

"Kidnapped!" Maceda exclaimed with a horrified look. "But who . . . and *why?*"

"We think the thief kidnapped Dad to stop his investigation," Joe explained. "And to pull off more thefts without the fear of being caught."

"Have you notified the police yet?" Justin asked.

Frank shook his head. "We'd rather keep the kidnapping quiet, at least for now," he said. "We're going to find our father, but at the same time, we want to catch the kidnapper. I'm worried that if he discovers the police are investigating, he'll find some way to escape."

"Well," Maceda said with a sigh, "since you're determined to carry out this investigation on your own, I feel I should help you out in any way I can. What can I do?"

34

"One thing we know for sure is that Dad's being held somewhere in the park," Frank told the architect.

"We'd like you to get us jobs here. As staff members, we'd be able to search every area of the park."

Maceda bit his lip and stared into space for a moment. "Yes," he said finally, turning his gaze back to Frank and Joe. "I think I can arrange internships for the two of you with Andrew. He'll be more likely to hire you if he doesn't have to pay you. He's extremely tight-fisted, as well as rude, demanding, and short-tempered."

"You don't like Mr. Taylor very much, do you?" Joe said as he and Frank followed the architect out the door.

"Let's just say we have different points of view regarding the Fourth Dimension," Maceda replied carefully. "I see it as a one-of-a-kind place where visitors can catch a glimpse of the future. He views it merely as a money-making operation."

Noting the bitterness in Maceda's voice as he talked about his boss, Frank was curious to see if Taylor really was the type of person Maceda had described.

When they reached Andrew Taylor's office, Maceda tapped gently on the door.

"Come in!" a voice inside the office snapped.

When they stepped into the large office, Frank recognized the tall, silver-haired man he and Joe had seen earlier in the hotel lobby. Taylor was sitting behind an expensive-looking, highly polished wooden desk, studying a computer printout.

Frank glanced around the office and saw that it was lined with bookcases and furnished with leather easy chairs, a sofa, and thick wall-to-wall carpeting.

"He's obviously not too tight-fisted when it comes to spending money on himself," Joe whispered to his brother.

Taylor looked up and took off his reading glasses, revealing a pair of piercing blue eyes. "I'm glad you're here, Justin," he said abruptly. "There's a problem we need to discuss." He waved his glasses at the Hardys. "Who are these kids?"

Frank felt his brother bristle with anger at being called a "kid." He put his hand on Joe's arm. "Chill out," he murmured. "We need him."

"Frank and Joe Hardy," Maceda told Taylor. "They would like to be interns here at the Fourth Dimension. Do you think you could find room for them? I will, of course, take full responsibility."

"Do they understand that they won't be paid?" Taylor asked sharply.

"Yes, Andrew," Maceda replied carefully.

"All right," Taylor said with a nod. "They're hired. I can always use the extra help, especially when it won't cost me anything." He looked at the Hardys coldly. "You'll work a nine to five day. Justin will tell you where to get uniforms and ID badges."

"Thanks, Mr. Taylor," Frank said. "We really appreciate this chance to learn about the Fourth Dimension."

Taylor ignored him and turned to Maceda. "What's this I hear about the new space shuttle simulator malfunctioning?" he asked.

"I . . . I'm sorry, Andrew," Justin said. "Once I reprogram the ride, it will work perfectly."

Taylor leaned forward and narrowed his eyes. "Like the jet pack ride that was supposed to work perfectly and totally failed?" he said, his voice rising with anger. "I pay you to design rides people can use, not prototypes that don't work. Every one of your failed experiments has cost me money!"

Frank looked at Maceda. The architect's face was pale, and he was staring down at the floor.

"I want that simulator in operation immediately," Taylor snapped. "That's all." He put his glasses back on and picked up the computer printout.

"Nice guy," Joe commented sarcastically as the three of them headed back to Maceda's office. "He's everything you said he was."

"He's nothing but a crass businessman," Justin muttered. He stopped and looked at the Hardys. "But that's not the worst of it," he fumed. "When the simulator is working again, Taylor will take credit for introducing an exciting, unique ride, the way he takes credit for all my work."

"Why don't you quit and get a job at another theme park?" Frank asked.

Maceda smiled sadly. "I couldn't do that, Frank. Remember, I designed the Fourth Dimension. It's become my home. I'd be lost anywhere else."

As soon as they arrived at Maceda's office, the phone began to ring. Maceda answered it and listened for a moment. Then he handed the cordless phone to Joe. "It's for you," he said.

Puzzled, Joe took the phone. "Joe Hardy," he said.

"That little realignment of the solar system was your first warning," came a rasping voice from the other end of the line. "This is your last. Don't interfere, and don't call the police. Nothing will happen to your father—or you—if you leave the Fourth Dimension *now*."

5 A Deadly Game

The caller hung up with a loud click. Joe pressed the Off button and silently handed the phone to Maceda.

"Well?" Frank asked. "Who was it?"

Joe told Frank and Maceda what the caller had said. Then he explained to Maceda what had happened at the monorail system earlier, when the model of the planet had crashed to the ground.

"Perhaps you'd better do as he says and leave the Fourth Dimension," Maceda said in a worried tone. "You could both be in real danger here."

"We're not leaving until we find Dad," Joe said stubbornly. "We can take care of ourselves."

"But there's your father's safety to consider as well," Maceda argued.

"We know that," Frank replied. "We'll just have to work quietly and quickly to get to Dad and catch the kidnapper before he decides to carry out his threat."

Just then, a beeping sound came from Justin's computer. He turned and looked at the screen, "Oh, dear," he said with a sigh. "The rock-o-matic chair in the Home of the Future is refusing to rock. Let's see if one of my programmers in the room out there corrects the problem."

A moment later, the beeping stopped. Maceda nodded with satisfaction. "It's working perfectly now.

"I could have solved the problem myself," he explained to the Hardys. "All the computers here are on one backbone, or network. But I let my programmers control the park's computerized rides and other attractions. That way, I can spend more time designing new attractions or perfecting older ones."

"We should probably let you get back to work, then," Frank said. "But before we leave, we need to ask you a few questions."

"Certainly," Maceda replied.

"Did you mention the stolen blueprints to Mike Strauss, and the fact that you hired Dad to get them back?" Frank asked him.

Maceda hesitated for a moment. "Yes, I did," he admitted finally. "I knew I could trust him with the information."

"We also need to know if Dad told you that we're

40

detectives," Joe said. "And whether or not you told Mr. Strauss about it."

"I believe I did mention it to Mike," Maceda said. He looked from Frank to Joe. "Why are you asking about all this? Is it important?"

"It might be," Joe replied. "Mike Strauss is our prime suspect so far."

"Mike!" Maceda exclaimed in surprise. "But why?"

"He knew about the theft and Dad's investigation," Frank explained. "He also knows who we are. So does the person who pushed the model planet and made that phone call. We only have Strauss's word that he was chloroformed. He could have made up the story as a cover for both the kidnapping and the safe robbery."

"Can you tell us anything about Strauss's background?" Joe asked Maceda.

"Only that he worked in a hotel in Chicago before coming here," Maceda said. "For some reason, he doesn't like to talk about that. I get the feeling he left there under bad circumstances."

"You mean he was fired?" Joe asked.

"It's possible," Maceda replied. "I really don't know. But I simply can't believe Mike Strauss is a thief and a kidnapper. However," he added, "I guess I can understand why you think he's a suspect."

"Just one more question," Frank said. "Those blueprints that were stolen from you—what were the designs for?"

41

"One was a blueprint for a new video game called Escape from the Labyrinth," Maceda told him. "The other was the design for a robot."

Frank nodded. "If we manage to find the blueprints during our investigation," he said as he and Joe turned to leave, "at least now we'll be able to identify them."

Maceda moved over to the door and opened it. "Andrew and I come up with daily assignments for the staff," he told them. "The assignments are posted on the bulletin board in the costume room in the basement of the theater. Heather Baker is in charge down there, and she'll find uniforms for you. I'll have a couple of staff ID badges sent over to you at the hotel later."

The Hardys thanked him and left the office. After they had stepped out of the Command Center, Frank said, "Let's head back to the hotel. I want to take a look at that video."

"Good idea," Joe said. "We can get an overall view of the park and the buildings we'll be searching."

When the brothers arrived at the hotel, they headed for the elevator. Frank was about to press the button when he heard a voice call out their names. They turned and saw Mike Strauss hurrying toward them. He was holding his mask in one hand. In his other hand was a small white envelope.

"I'm glad I caught you," the hotel manager said breathlessly, holding out the envelope. "A man left this for you at the desk. It's marked urgent."

"What did the guy look like?" Joe asked, taking it from Strauss.

"He was about sixty, short, and a little heavyset, with a bushy white beard," Strauss reported. "I think he stayed here before, but I can't remember his name. So many guests come and go here, it's hard to remember everyone's name."

At that moment, the elevator doors opened and out stepped a slim young woman with braided black hair wearing a chambermaid's uniform. The Hardys walked past her into the elevator.

"I hope you found your badge, Meg," Frank heard Strauss say to the young woman. Turning sharply, Frank pressed the Door Open button just as the elevator doors were about to close. He stepped out of the elevator and approached Strauss and the young woman. Puzzled, Joe followed his brother.

"I'm sorry, Mike," Meg was saying. "My badge just seems to have disappeared."

"Well, you're new here, so I'll overlook your carelessness this time," Strauss told her. "I'll get you another badge, but if you lose that one, the cost of replacing it will have to come out of your salary." He turned and walked off toward the reception desk.

"Excuse me," Frank said to Meg. "Can I ask you a question?"

The young woman turned to face him. "Sure," she said, "but make it quick. I have to get back to work."

43

"Is there another chambermaid at the hotel named Meg?" Frank asked her. "Blond, with glasses?"

"No way," Meg replied, shaking her head. "I've been working at the Galaxy for a week, and I've met all the other chambermaids. I'm the only Meg around here, and I've never had to wear glasses."

"When did you first discover your badge was missing?" Joe asked her.

"At around nine-thirty this morning," Meg answered, "when my roommate and I got to the chambermaids' dressing room in the hotel basement. The badge is always pinned to my uniform, and I saw that it was gone. I've spent almost the whole day looking for it."

Meg looked confused. "Why are you asking me about my missing badge?"

"We, uh, found one," Frank said. "But now I remember—the name on that badge was Megan, not Meg. Sorry to waste your time."

Meg gave an exasperated sigh. "Well, if you *do* happen to come across *my* badge with *my* name on it, would you turn it in at the desk?" she said impatiently.

"Absolutely," Frank replied, moving over to the elevator and pressing the button.

"You know what this means," he said to Joe after the elevator doors had closed behind them.

Joe nodded. "The chambermaid who was cleaning Dad's room this morning must have been a fake."

"Right." Frank nodded. "So now we have two suspects—Strauss and this mystery woman. Do you think they're working together?"

The elevator had reached the ninth floor. The Hardys stepped out and walked down the hallway to their room.

"It makes sense," Joe said as he unlocked the door. "Strauss could have hired someone to pose as a chambermaid. She packed up Dad's stuff and cleared away traces of the kidnapping. Strauss could have done it right after the kidnapping, but maybe he was afraid of making too much noise and arousing suspicion. So he had the maid do it the next morning."

Frank motioned toward the envelope Joe was holding. "Let's take a look at what's in there."

Joe ripped open the sealed envelope and pulled out a folded-up piece of paper. He unfolded it and saw that it was a handwritten note on hotel stationery.

"'I need to talk to you tomorrow morning about Fenton Hardy,'" Joe read out loud. "'I'll find you.' It's signed 'E. Brody.'"

"E. Brody," Frank said slowly. "Why does that name sound familiar?" He took the note from Joe and looked at it. "I've definitely seen that name somewhere," he murmured, shaking his head.

Just then there was a knock at the door. Joe opened it and saw Laurel Kramer standing in the hall.

"Justin asked me to drop these off," she said,

45

reaching into her purse and pulling out two metallic ID badges. "Can I come in for a minute?" she added. "There's something I want to talk to you about."

"Sure," Joe said, opening the door wider.

Laurel stepped into the room and handed the badges to Joe. "I'm very concerned about Justin," she said. "Not only is he upset by the theft of his blueprints, but Taylor has been on his case constantly. Justin's agreed to take full responsibility for you as interns, and I don't want him to have to take any heat from Taylor if you two don't work out here. So just don't mess up, okay?"

With that, she turned and left the room, closing the door behind her.

Joe gave a low whistle. "Talk about a loyal assistant," he said. He looked at his brother. "What are you thinking, Frank?"

"I'm thinking that if Maceda told her about the theft of his blueprints, maybe he also told her about hiring Dad and the fact that we're detectives. That might make her a suspect."

"Do you think *she's* the mystery chambermaid?" Joe asked.

"That's what we have to find out." He glanced at his watch. "Let's get some dinner and watch that video. Tomorrow we'll continue our search for Dad."

Joe nodded. "This is one job we definitely *can't* mess up."

* * *

The next morning, when Frank and Joe arrived at the theater, they took the elevator down to the basement. When the doors opened, the Hardys found themselves looking into a large room filled with costumes, masks, and wigs worn by characters from science-fiction movies, comics, and TV shows. Staff members were busy choosing costumes from racks and trying them on in dressing rooms.

"This place is awesome," Joe said as they passed a rack of white star-fighter outfits from a well-known science-fiction TV show.

Frank and Joe found the bulletin board on the wall between the dressing rooms. "We're supposed to take part in something called the Space War Gladiator Game at the arena this morning," Joe said, pointing at the board. "At three-thirty, we have to report to the Video Arcade to assist visitors who want to play virtual reality games."

The Hardys approached the desk where Heather Baker, the person in charge of costumes, was sitting. After Frank had told her what their first assignment was, she led them across the room to a rack of gold-colored spandex pants and tops. A black lightning stripe zigzagged across the front and back of the long-sleeved shirts. On the floor under the rack were several pairs of black canvas boots.

"These are the interns' uniforms," Heather explained. "But you also can wear them for the gladiator games. The gladiators' armor and helmets are in the bin next to the clothing rack. Let me know if you need help with sizes," she said before heading back to her desk.

Frank and Joe selected uniforms and gladiator gear, headed into the dressing room, and began to change into their outfits.

"I hope this game doesn't take too long," Joe muttered as he tied armor made out of heavy black plastic around his chest. "We're wasting time doing this when we should be searching for Dad." He picked up his helmet and placed it on his head. Then he stood next to his brother in front of the full-length mirror.

"Do we look weird, or what?" Joe said.

Both brothers were wearing shiny black chest and leg armor over their yellow interns' uniforms. Their black helmets had eye holes and covered most of their faces, leaving only their mouths and chins exposed.

"We look okay—for space gladiators," Frank said. "So let's go play some gladiator games."

The Hardys headed for the elevator, which had just arrived. The doors were about to close when a young, tall man with very short dark hair wearing a star-fighter costume hurried into the elevator. He nodded briefly at the Hardys but didn't say anything. Frank glanced at the young man's ID badge and saw that his name was Steve Willis.

Suddenly there was a faint beeping sound, and Frank saw Willis lift his left wrist and press a button on his watch. It was an unusual-looking watch,

Frank thought. He'd never seen a red watch with a black, star-shaped dial before.

The elevator came to a stop on the first floor, and the brothers left the theater and headed for the arena, a large, domed building in the middle of the park. Inside the arena, Frank and Joe found four staffers in gladiator costumes waiting for them.

"My name is Mark Hoffman," one of the men told Frank and Joe. "Your fellow gladiators are Greg, Josh, and Sue," he added, pointing to each of them in turn. "The audience arrives in half an hour for the performance. Before that, I need to explain the game to you. Then we'll have a short rehearsal."

Mark pointed to the center of the arena. "As you can see, the arena is filled with five-foot-high platforms, with steps, jagged craters filled with water, and boulders of different shapes and sizes. The floor is carpeted to prevent injuries. The object of the game is to zap your opponent with your 'laser' gun while avoiding being zapped yourself. If you get zapped three times, you're out of the game. The next gladiator takes over."

He handed each of them a silver-colored gun. Joe thought it looked and felt like a long, heavy drill.

"The gun doesn't shoot a real laser beam," Mark explained. "It shoots a beam of light, like a flashlight, and makes a high-pitched pinging noise when the light hits the target. Okay," he said, "who wants to go first?"

"I will," Frank offered.

49

"And I'll be his opponent," Sue said, stepping forward.

"Okay," Mark said. "Find yourselves some hiding places."

Sue quickly stationed herself behind one of the platforms, gun in hand. Frank noticed that her gun was black, not silver-colored.

Frank moved behind an eight-foot-high boulder. He heard Mark count to three and shout, "Go!"

Frank saw Sue dart out from behind the platform. He moved out from his hiding place cautiously, aimed, and fired. Immediately he heard the pinging sound and saw a beam of light hit the woman's armor.

"Good," he heard Mark say. "But you both need to keep moving."

Frank scurried across the floor and crouched down behind a boulder. He raised himself up a little and peered over the top of the rock. Sue was standing about ten feet away, on top of a platform, her gun pointed straight at him. She fired.

Frank dropped down behind the boulder. At the same time, he heard a hissing sound behind him. He turned and saw a small, burning hole in the carpet. Suddenly, the truth hit him. His opponent was using a gun with a real—and deadly—laser beam!

6 Followed

"Hey, what's going on here?" Mark shouted as Frank's attacker dropped her weapon and ran past Joe toward the arena exit.

"Don't let her get away," Frank yelled. "She has a real laser gun." But Joe had already taken off after the woman. When he was out of the arena, he pulled off his helmet so he could see better. Suddenly, he spotted her. She was heading for a large crowd near the Sci-Fi Exhibit. The crowd was watching a demonstration of a hovercraft car, a sleek black sports car that could lift off the ground and move through the air.

When Frank caught up with Joe, he pulled off his helmet. "We've got to catch her before we lose her in that crowd," he said desperately. "That laser gun could have seriously hurt someone."

The brothers shot forward, but by the time they reached the tightly packed crowd of people, Frank's attacker had disappeared. The Hardys scanned the crowd, hoping to catch a glimpse of the slim young woman, but it was no use.

"I can't believe we lost her," Joe said as they headed back to the arena. "I don't like this, Frank. It's the second attack. Who knows how far the kidnappers will go to keep us from finding Dad."

"That's a risk we'll have to take," Frank said grimly. "But at least we know for sure now that a woman was involved in the kidnapping."

Joe nodded, "And I'd be willing to bet that Sue isn't her real name."

When they got back to the arena, they saw Mark standing on the sidelines testing the guns of the three remaining gladiators. The black laser gun used by Frank's attacker was lying on the floor next to him.

"None of these silver-colored guns are real laser guns," Mark said to Frank and Joe.

Frank picked up the black gun. "Do you know where this came from?" he asked Mark.

"All the guns are supposed to come from the prop room in the costume area," Mark replied. "But when Sue arrived here, she was already carrying that gun. I have no idea where she managed to get it." He shook his head. "I can't believe it. Why would she be stupid enough to play a practical joke like that?"

"That's what we'd like to know," Joe said. He wasn't about to tell Mark, but he was sure that the attack on Frank was no joke. "What do you know about that woman?"

"I've never met her before," Mark admitted. "She must be new here. She just showed up a few minutes before you did and said she was filling in for Kathy, one of my regulars who's been out with the flu. Sue didn't give me her last name. I'll contact Justin and ask him about her. He keeps all the personnel files."

Just then, a crowd of visitors began arriving at the arena. Mark glanced at his watch. "It's nearly show time," he said. He looked at Frank and Joe. "I know you had a bad experience before, but would you mind sticking around and playing the game? I really need you guys. And you looked good out there, Frank."

"Yeah, but wait till you see *my* dodge and strike strategy," Joe said, grinning. "I plan to win this game."

Frank rolled his eyes. "My brother isn't exactly Mr. Modest," he said to Mark.

"I'm sure you'll both give the crowd a show to remember," Mark said with a laugh.

When the game was over, the Hardys walked back to the theater to drop off their equipment. Both Hardys had taken off their helmets and armor.

"See? I told you I'd win," Joe said smugly. "It's all a matter of timing."

"Yeah, right," Frank shot back. "Timing and the fact that your opponent tripped and fell into a crater filled with water." Suddenly he stopped and turned his head sharply to glance over his shoulder.

"What's going on?" Joe demanded. "You've been looking for something ever since we left the arena."

"We're being followed," Frank told him. "By a short, older man with white hair and a bushy white beard. Look over there."

Joe glanced over his shoulder and saw the guy his brother had described. The small man scurried out from behind one of the pillars that lined the sidewalk and made his way to the pillar in front of it. He peeked out from behind the pillar, glimpsed the Hardys staring in his direction, and immediately pulled his head out of sight.

"He's not doing a very good job of tailing us," Joe commented. "Hey, wait a minute," he said suddenly. "Isn't that Brody, the guy Strauss described? The one who wrote the note?"

Frank nodded. "That's the guy. Come on," he said, "let's find out what he's up to."

The brothers approached the man. He had his back to the pillar, and he was looking away from Frank and Joe.

"Okay, Mr. Brody, the hide-and-seek game is over," Joe said, a smirk on his face.

Brody gave a nervous start, then turned his head

slowly toward Frank and Joe. His expression relaxed, and he smiled at the brothers.

"Well, well," he said with a chuckle. "I said I'd find you, but it turns out that you found me first. Frank and Joe Hardy, I presume."

"Correct," Frank said. "But how do you know who we are?"

"I live in Bayport," Brody replied. "I know your father, and I've seen you two around town. I own a business on Main Street."

"That's right," Frank said suddenly. "Now I know why your name sounds familiar. You're Ernest Brody, and you own Brody Building Supply."

"That's me," the short man said, smiling. "But I've retired. My son handles the business now."

"Why were you following us, Mr. Brody?" Joe asked.

Brody smiled at him. "The truth is I've always been a big fan of mystery stories," he explained. "I know that you and your brother are detectives, so I thought I'd try to tail you. How'd I do?" he asked, looking at Frank and Joe hopefully.

"Uh, okay," Joe said. He didn't want to hurt the older man's feelings. "But next time, you need to do a better job of concealing yourself."

Brody sighed. "I guess it takes practice."

"I think we'd better get to the point of this meeting," Frank said. "Mr. Brody, your note said you needed to talk to us about our father."

"Yes," Brody said, nodding. "But why don't we

discuss it over lunch? There's a restaurant near the Science-Fiction Exhibit called the Interstellar Snack Shop."

"Okay with us," Joe said.

Brody led them to a small building shaped like an astronaut's helmet. Inside the building were tables and the kitchen. Tables were also set up in a pavilion outside the restaurant.

Frank and Joe saw that the crowd outside the Sci-Fi Exhibit had left. But a driver in a leather jumpsuit and helmet was still demonstrating the hovercraft car to a few people. Joe saw the car's convertible top slowly slide down from the front of the vehicle to the back.

The Hardys and Brody sat down at one of the tables and picked up menus.

"'Vegetarian Space Flight Special—Corn, Carrot, Bean, and Zucchini Paste—Served in Individual Silver Tubes,'" Joe read aloud. "Is this menu some sort of joke?"

"You'll find regular food on the menu, too," Brody said, chuckling. "But I've had that vegetarian dish here before, and it's really quite tasty. I'm going to order it again."

"I think I'll stick to a burger and fries," Joe said.

When they had given their order to a waiter in a spacesuit, Brody leaned toward the Hardys. "When I got your message on my answering machine," he said, "I thought I'd better catch the next flight down here. I was worried that something might have gone wrong with the investigation."

"I don't get it," Joe said, frowning. "How are you involved in Dad's investigation?"

Brody looked startled. "Didn't you know?" he asked. "I hired Fenton to investigate a scam operation going on here at the Fourth Dimension."

Frank and Joe stared in amazement at Brody, then looked quizzically at each other.

"We didn't know Dad was investigating two cases," Frank said. He told Brody how their father asked them to meet him at the Fourth Dimension and what had happened since they arrived.

When Frank finished, Brody sat with a stunned expression on his face. "Kidnapped," he whispered, shaking his head. "I can't believe it."

"Maybe you'd better tell us what you know about this scam operation," Frank prodded.

The waiter arrived with the food. After he left, Brody said, "It all started last month. I came down here for a vacation and met several other retirees.

"A few days after I arrived," Brody continued, "I was approached in my hotel room by a young man and woman who said they were real estate developers selling affordable condos at New Dimension Retirement Village near the Fourth Dimension.

"I have no intention of ever leaving Bayport," Brody went on, "but I must admit, I was curious to see what the condos looked like. But when I asked the developers to show them to me, they claimed that construction had just started and it would be a while before a model home would be available for viewing. They did show me the site from a hotel window and a brochure with an illustration of the condos. They also insisted that, because of their excellent price, buyers were snapping up the condos sight unseen."

"Did you believe that?" Joe asked, pouring ketchup on his fries.

"Well, I later learned that two of the couples I had met actually *did* give the developers deposits —ten percent of the total condo price. They were afraid they'd miss out on a great deal," Brody replied. "But I was suspicious of the operation, so I visited the construction site on my own. It's about a quarter-mile outside the park."

Frank nodded. "We can see it from our hotel room."

"There were no builders on the site when I got there," Brody continued. "Just an empty construction trailer, a bulldozer, and a small sign that said, Commercial Zoning Permit, Number 346. That's when I realized the operation was a scam. If the site is zoned for business, it can't be used for private dwellings like condos. I wanted to warn my new friends, but they had already left the park. I know their names, but I don't know where they live," he added with a grimace.

"Do you remember the names of the developers?" Joe asked, remembering the piece of paper he and Frank had found in their father's room.

"They introduced themselves as Daniel Doherty and Susan Howell, owners of Doherty-Howell Development Company," Brody replied.

Frank suddenly noticed a long line of people outside the pavilion waiting for tables.

"We'd better leave," he told the others. "A lot of people are waiting."

They paid the check and left the restaurant. When they reached the sidewalk, the Hardys and Brody spotted the hovercraft car. It was flying about five feet above the ground, circling a fountain in the middle of a grassy area near the clock tower.

The three of them turned and started to walk south, toward the theater. A few moments later, Frank realized the older man wasn't beside him. Frank looked over his shoulder and saw that Brody had stopped several feet back and was kneeling down to tie his shoelaces.

Then Frank heard a whirring sound and spotted the hovercraft car coming in their direction. There were shrieks of fear and shouts of anger as people jumped out of the vehicle's way. Brody heard the noise and straightened up, a puzzled expression on his face.

The sleek, black car suddenly picked up speed and swerved to the left. Joe cried out, "Watch your heads!"

Frank gasped as he saw that the driver was heading straight for Brody!

7 A Near Miss

"Get down!" Frank cried as he sprinted toward Brody. Frank grabbed his arm and pulled the startled man to the ground, out of the path of the hovercraft car.

The helmeted driver flew the convertible car over Frank and Brody, then swerved toward Joe. But instead of dodging the vehicle, the younger Hardy dropped his armor and helmet, grabbed onto the edge of the passenger door, and began to pull himself inside the vehicle.

"Mind if I hitch a ride?" Joe asked as he began to swing his left leg over the door.

Joe couldn't see the driver's face through the visor on the man's helmet, but he heard the driver say, "Sure. I'll take you for the ride of your life."

The driver accelerated, and the hovercraft climbed to seven feet and banked sharply to the right. Then the helmeted man reached out a gloved hand and released the door handle. The door swung open, leaving Joe hanging in midair. Joe's feet grazed over some bushes, and he gripped the door tightly as the driver flew swiftly through the park.

People stopped to stare at the sight of the hovercraft whizzing by with Joe hanging from the open door. The ground flew by so quickly that Joe saw only a green blur. He had to swing his legs upward as the car flew right over a sign that stood about five feet tall.

Suddenly, Joe saw that they were rapidly approaching a shade tree. Seconds before he was about to slam into one of the tree's branches, Joe released his grip and dropped to the ground. He lay on the grass, stunned. As the hovercraft raced away, the open door slammed into the tree and then closed with a loud whack.

Frank rushed over to his brother. Brody followed at a slower pace, carrying Joe's armor and helmet. "Are you okay?" Frank asked, kneeling down beside his brother.

Joe took some deep breaths and immediately began to feel better. "Yeah, I'm okay," he said as he slowly got to his feet. "I'm just mad that I couldn't stop that guy." He glanced around the park. "Where'd he go, anyway?"

"He took off over a low section of the roller

coaster," Brody reported. "He's out of the park."

"Well, I don't think we should waste time looking for him," Frank said. "I'm sure he knows this area better than we do. He'll land and disappear before we can find him."

"Did you get a look at him?" Brody asked Joe.

Joe shook his head. "His face was totally covered by his visor." He paused for a moment. "But there's one thing I *do* know, Mr. Brody. You've got to leave the Fourth Dimension as soon as possible. You're in danger here."

"Joe's right," Frank said, nodding. "You were the main target of that attack. The kidnappers must have recognized you as one of their scam victims, and now they think you're working with us. They may come after you again."

"I'll take my chances," Brody said firmly. "I'm Fenton's client, and I'm determined to stay and help you find him. Nothing you can say will change my decision."

The brothers looked at each other and shrugged. There was obviously no point in arguing with the older man. His mind was made up.

"Okay," Frank said to Brody. "But you've got to be totally alert wherever you go in the park—you even have to be careful in your hotel room."

"Especially in there," Joe added. "Mike Strauss, the hotel manager, is our prime suspect." He turned to his brother. "What do you think? Was Dad investigating two cases? Are the kidnappers thieves or scam artists—or both? And if we're just dealing with scam artists, does that mean Justin Maceda made up the story about the stolen blueprints to put us on the wrong track?"

"Maceda could have been lying," Frank said slowly. "But I can't see why he would involve himself in a scam operation."

"What did the developers look like?" Joe asked Brody.

"Doherty wore a dark green sports jacket and was about six feet tall, with long, curly red hair and a red beard," Brody replied promptly. "Susan Howell was a young woman, about five-seven, with short blond hair and brown eyes. I remember that she was wearing a turtleneck sweater."

"Strauss is around six feet," Joe said. "But he doesn't have red hair or a beard. Our mystery chambermaid had long hair and glasses."

"The scammers were probably in disguise," Frank pointed out. "That way the scam victims wouldn't be able to make a positive ID. They may even use different names at different times."

"What about our other suspect, Laurel Kramer?" Joe wondered aloud. "How does she fit in now?"

"She doesn't," Frank said. "Except that the gladiator who attacked me was a woman and so is one of the scammers. But Kramer did mention the supposedly stolen blueprints. It's possible that Maceda told her to mention them to us to distract us. That way we wouldn't investigate the real crime—the scam operation."

"I still think Strauss is our strongest suspect," Joe said. "He could have made up the robbery story to cover up his role in the kidnapping. Maybe he, Maceda, and Kramer are working together."

"What we need are some solid clues that will help us find Dad and catch the kidnappers," Frank said with frustration.

"So let's start searching for some," Joe said. "I want to take a look at the fire stairs on our floor. Maybe the kidnappers took Dad out that way. The security person we talked to said that the hotel service entrance was guarded, but she didn't mention the fire exits."

"Good thinking," Frank said. "And while you're doing that, I'll try to search Strauss's office."

"What should I do?" Brody asked eagerly.

"See if you can spot the people posing as developers who approached you. Maybe they're wearing the same disguises and you'll recognize them. But be careful."

"And if you *do* see them, don't try to follow them," Joe cautioned. "Call us first, okay?"

Brody nodded, then smiled at the Hardys. "Well, what are we waiting for? Let's get to work."

The Hardys dropped off their armor and helmets at the costume room before returning to the hotel. "Don't forget," Joe said as they were leaving the theater. "We're supposed to meet Laurel Kramer at the Video Arcade at three-thirty."

Frank looked at his watch. "That gives us an hour to investigate. We'd better get started."

When the Hardys got to the hotel, they split up. Joe headed up to the ninth floor. First he searched the hallway between his father's room and the fire stairs. Then he carefully checked out the stairs in case the kidnappers had left any clues behind that might identify them. But he reached the ground floor without finding anything.

Joe pushed open the metal fire door and stepped out of the building. He found himself standing in a driveway that curved around the hotel toward the service entrance. To the left was a high concrete wall with an arched opening that led into the park.

There was a dumpster standing a few feet away from Joe. He glanced at it and saw that one of the black garbage bags inside was ripped. The sleeve of a sweater was visible where the bag was torn. The pattern on the sweater looked familiar to Joe. He stepped over to the dumpster, pulled the sweater out of the bag, and held it up.

"I knew I recognized this sweater," he murmured. "It's Dad's."

Joe tied the sweater around his waist and began to search through the garbage bag. He found more of his father's belongings, including Fenton's laptop computer and his glasses case. Under the glasses case, Joe spotted a staff ID badge with the name Meg on it.

Joe took the computer and the glasses case out of

the bag, but left the badge inside. If I return the badge, he thought, Strauss will know where I found it and figure out that we're on his trail.

He shoved the garbage bag deep into the dumpster, then went back to the hotel. Climbing the stairs to the ninth floor, he let himself into his room. He opened his suitcase and placed the computer and sweater inside. He was about to do the same with the glasses case when he noticed that there was a folded piece of paper inside it. He pulled it out and unfolded it.

"It's a map of the park," he said in a surprised tone. He looked at the map more closely and saw that four buildings on it had been circled. "That's strange," he muttered, shaking his head. "Just what were you up to, Dad?"

Joe shoved the map into his pocket, dropped the glasses case into his suitcase, and zipped the bag shut. He looked at his watch. He had fifteen minutes to get to the Video Arcade.

Frank sneaked into a phone booth in an alcove several feet away from the reception desk. He pretended to dial phone numbers while he waited for an opportunity to get into Mike Strauss's office.

Finally he got his chance. He saw the hotel manager place a folded card on the desk and head toward the elevator with three men in staff uniforms.

As soon as Frank saw the elevator doors close, he left the phone booth and walked quickly across the

66

lobby to the reception desk. He glanced at the card. "'Please call Room 1506 for manager,'" he read. Making his way around the desk, he tried the door. Much to his surprise, it wasn't locked. He stepped into Strauss's office, closed the door gently behind him, and looked around. Besides the desk and safe, the office contained a file cabinet.

Frank checked the file cabinet and then searched the desk drawers, hoping to find evidence that would incriminate Strauss. He had opened the bottom right-hand drawer and was searching through a stack of papers when he suddenly spotted a letter with the address of a well-known, expensive Chicago hotel printed at the top. Frank pulled out the letter and began to read.

The letter warned Strauss that if he didn't continue to pay back money he had stolen from the hotel safe, legal action would be taken. The letter also stated that Strauss still owed the hotel fifty thousand dollars. It was signed by the hotel's manager.

"Well, what do you know," Frank said to himself. "Strauss definitely needs a lot of money—and fast. I wonder if he's running the scam operation to get it."

He replaced the letter and shut the drawer. As he straightened up, he saw that the clock on Strauss's desk read three-twenty. Frank quickly left the office and headed upstairs to his room to get his jacket.

He was about to leave the room when he heard talking and laughing sounds. He looked to his left and saw a tall, red-haired young man and a young blond woman come out of a room a few doors down the hall. Frank gasped in amazement. The young man and woman looked exactly like the phony developers Ernest Brody had described.

Frank shut the door until it was only open a crack. Then he peered through the crack and saw an older couple follow the younger man and woman out the door.

"You won't regret this," Frank heard the red-haired man say. "You're going to love living at New Dimension."

"You'll be receiving a call from our lawyer within thirty days," the young woman said. "And it won't be long before you can visit a model home on the site."

"Oh, how wonderful," the older woman said. She turned to her husband. "Just think, dear. Soon we'll be living in our very own condo in a beautiful retirement village!"

The four of them shook hands, and the younger couple got on the elevator. Frank waited until the elevator doors had closed before he bolted out of the room and caught the other elevator on the floor. He reached the lobby just as the red-haired man and blond woman were heading out the door. The woman stepped into the monorail station, but the man kept walking northeast in the direction of the Science-Fiction Exhibit.

For a moment, Frank wasn't sure whom he should

follow. Then he made up his mind and took off after the man.

When the man reached the Science-Fiction Exhibit, he entered the building. Frank followed him inside and saw him start up a flight of stairs. He waited a moment to make sure the man wouldn't see him, then went up the stairs after him.

He saw the man unlock a metal door marked No Admittance and disappear through it. Frank bolted up the stairs and caught the door before it clicked shut. As he peered into the room, he saw the red-bearded man step behind a black velvet curtain.

Frank rushed over to the curtain and pulled it aside. As he did, there was a puff of smoke, and the man he'd been chasing vanished from sight!

8 Up in Smoke

Frank stared in astonishment at the empty space where the red-haired man had just stood moments before. The smoke cleared, and he saw a semicircular glass capsule. Set in the floor of the capsule was a black metal disk large enough for a person to stand on. Against the back wall of the capsule was a control panel with three buttons, none of which were marked.

Frank saw a thin space between the disk and the platform and realized that the man had disappeared down a mini-elevator. Stepping onto the disk, Frank pressed one of the buttons. Nothing happened. He tried the other two buttons, but the elevator wouldn't budge.

Frank turned and raced back down the stairs,

70

hoping to catch up with the man. But when he reached the ground floor, there was no sign of the red-haired, bearded man among the crowd of people at the exhibit.

Frank hurried over to a staffer who was standing near the building's entrance directing visitors to different exhibits.

"Excuse me," Frank said to the young woman. "Did you see a red-haired guy with a red beard wearing a dark green jacket leave the building during the past five minutes or so?"

She thought for a moment, then shook her head. "I don't remember seeing anyone like that," she said. "He must have left by the fire exit over there." She pointed past a standing display of sci-fi movie posters to a red exit sign at the back of the main room.

"Is that where the elevators are?" Frank asked her. "Back there?"

"This building doesn't have any elevators," the young woman told him. "There are only two floors. Besides, the second-floor exhibit isn't even finished. It's supposed to be a replica of a starship's transporter room from a famous TV series. Laurel Kramer was working on it a few months ago, but I heard that she was having trouble with the design, so the project was scrapped."

At that moment, a couple with three young children came up to the young woman and began to ask her for directions.

Frank left the building and headed for the monorail stop nearby. As he rode the train to the Video Arcade, he tried to make sense out of what the woman had told him. If there aren't any elevators in that building, then where did the mini-elevator take that guy, he wondered. Was it just a coincidence that Laurel Kramer designed an elevator that was being used by one of the scam artists? Or did she design it specifically for the scammers? By the time he reached the stop at the Video Arcade he still had no answers.

When Frank stepped into the arcade, he spotted his brother playing a video game. He walked over to Joe and saw that the game he was playing was Mega Baseball.

"You're down to your last out," Frank said, peering down over his brother's shoulder.

"I know that," Joe snapped. He pushed some buttons and the words *Game Over* flashed on the screen. "Rats," Joe shouted, hitting the machine with the palm of his hand.

"Hey, chill out," Frank said. "It's only a game."

"It's not that," Joe shot back. "I've been wasting almost an hour waiting for you and Laurel Kramer to show up. I should have been checking this building for clues. I know we aren't sure if Kramer's still a suspect, but I didn't want her to catch me snooping around, just in case." He looked at his brother. "I'm worried about Dad, Frank. I just want to find him. These intern jobs are taking up too much time."

"I know," Frank said. "And I'm sorry I'm late. But I did find some clues that might bring us closer to identifying the kidnappers. Trouble is," he added, "I can't make sense of some of them." He told his brother what he'd found in Strauss's office and what had happened at the hotel and Science-Fiction Exhibit.

"I think it's definitely suspicious that Laurel Kramer designed a mini-elevator used by one of the scam artists," Joe said after Frank finished. "Wait a minute," he said suddenly. "What if she was the woman scammer you saw? Maybe she's late because she had to get rid of her disguise."

"It's possible," Frank said. "But we need more evidence. She could be late for lots of reasons. Did you come up with any clues at the hotel?"

Joe told him about finding the garbage bag with their father's belongings and the map.

"I didn't have time to take a look at the buildings Dad circled on the map," Joe said. "We need to do that and also to check out the laptop computer. There may be information about the case on it."

"Unless the kidnappers erased it," Frank pointed out.

Just then, Frank heard a man's voice call out their names. He looked over at the arcade entrance. Coming toward them was Steve Willis, the dark-haired young man with the star-shaped watch who had ridden in the costume room elevator earlier with Frank and Joe. Willis had changed from his star-fighter costume into a light blue and black staff uniform similar in style to the outfits the Hardys wore.

"I'm Steve Willis," the young man said. "Didn't I see you guys on the costume room elevator this morning?"

"Right," Frank replied. "I'm Frank Hardy, and this is my brother, Joe."

"Nice to meet you," Willis said, smiling. "I'm sorry I'm late. I was conducting a tour of the Biosphere and people were asking me a lot of questions about how it works."

He led the Hardys over to a table set up against the wall. Frank and Joe saw two helmets with earphones and large, black visors sitting on the table. The helmets and two sets of handheld controls were attached by long wires to a computer.

"This computer is programmed to play two virtual reality video games," Willis explained to them. "Do you guys know what virtual reality is?"

"Sure," Frank replied. "The computer sends the game to a screen in the helmet's visor. Players actually feel as if they are inside the game moving from place to place."

"Right," Willis said with an approving nod. "The person at the computer controls what the player encounters in the game and the sound effects. And this," he added, picking up one of the handheld controls, "allows the player to either zap, jump over, or go around any aliens, monsters, or obstacles."

Just then a boy and girl, who looked about twelve,

came up to them. "Can my cousin and I play one of those games?" the boy asked.

"Definitely," Willis told him. "But first we need to give the game a test run to see if it's working right. Why don't you watch me work the computer while you're waiting." He turned to Frank and Joe. "Who's going to try out the game?"

"I'll do it," Frank offered.

Steve Willis handed him one of the helmets, then turned to the computer. "Nod when you're ready to begin," Willis said. "By the way, the game is called Dragonfire."

Frank placed the helmet over his head and felt someone hand him a set of controls. He nodded. Seconds later, a colorized scene flashed before his eyes, and he saw that he was in the middle of a large room in a medieval castle. Frank had a growing feeling of excitement. It was as though he were really walking down a wide corridor.

Suddenly, a knight on a horse came charging toward him. The knight was yelling and holding a long, pointed lance. Frank pushed the joystick forward. The image of the knight shimmered, then disappeared, but the horse continued to gallop toward Frank. The sound of the pounding hooves got louder and louder as the animal approached. It reared up right in front of him and whinnied loudly. Frank instinctively ducked his head to avoid the horse. Then he pushed the joystick to the right and felt himself moving around the animal.

The scene shifted to a forest. Fog swirled around

huge rocks, and the branches of weeping willow trees hung down like ghostly figures. As Frank jumped across a small ravine and moved through the misty forest, he heard dead leaves crunching under his feet, owls hooting, and the sound of crickets. A bird of prey let loose an ear-splitting screech.

Then came a sudden deafening roar, and an enormous dragon rose straight out of the mist. The dragon headed straight for Frank, flames shooting out of its mouth. Frank took a few steps backward in an attempt to avoid the noise. The roars grew louder and louder as the dragon loomed larger and larger.

Frank pushed the joystick frantically, but nothing happened. It seemed to be useless in controlling the game. He began to feel dizzy from the ear-splitting noise and the huge image of the dragon, now only inches away.

He dropped the controls and fell to his knees, his hands clutching the helmet. "Stop!" he yelled, collapsing onto the floor. "The noise is killing me!"

9 Virtual Reality

The noise inside the helmet stopped, except for the ringing in Frank's ears. He felt the helmet being lifted off his head, and he opened his eyes to see his brother staring down at him anxiously.

"Are you all right?" Joe asked, placing the helmet on the floor.

Frank nodded and got to his feet. As he did, he saw several kids standing nearby gaping at him. A woman hurried up to the boy and girl who had asked about the game earlier. "Come on, kids, we're leaving," she snapped. "These games are just too dangerous."

The Hardys and Willis watched as the woman hustled the boy and girl out of the arcade. Then

Willis turned to Frank and asked, "Did something go wrong with the game?"

"It turned out to be a little too real," Frank replied. He described what had happened.

"I'm really sorry about that," Willis said. "The game shouldn't have malfunctioned. I'd better check the program. I'll see you guys later, okay?" He turned to the computer and began typing some commands.

"Are you thinking what I'm thinking?" Joe said as he and Frank left the arcade.

"Probably," Frank said grimly. "You're wondering whether Willis might have programmed that game to malfunction himself, right?"

Joe nodded.

"Well, there's no way to tell for sure right now," Frank said. "But it's definitely something to think about."

Joe looked at his watch. "It's nearly five-thirty," he said. "We'd better head back to the hotel and take a look at Dad's computer and that map."

"Good idea," Frank said. Then he sighed and shook his head.

"What's wrong?" Joe asked.

"I was just thinking about Dad," Frank said. "I hope he's okay. He's probably wondering when we're going to get around to finding him."

"That makes two of us," Joe said grimly.

Fifteen minutes later, Frank and Joe were back in their room. Joe was sitting on his bed studying the map. Frank was at the desk typing on his father's laptop computer.

"I don't get it," Joe said, frowning. "The four buildings Dad circled are the Science-Fiction Exhibit, the Space Flight Building, Hall of Holograms, and the Home of the Future. Why did he do that?"

"Maybe he found something in each of those buildings," Frank said over his shoulder. "We'll definitely need to check them out. I just wish I had some idea what we're supposed to be looking for."

He stopped typing and turned to face Joe. "There's nothing on the computer about the case," he reported. "Either the kidnappers erased it or Dad never entered any information." He stood up from the desk and stretched. "Let's go get some dinner at the Interstellar Snack Shop and plan our next move."

When the Hardys reached the lobby, Frank nudged his brother. "See that older couple sitting on the sofa drinking iced tea?" he said. "That's the couple I saw talking with the scam artists earlier. Let's go talk to them."

The brothers approached the couple and introduced themselves.

"I'm Jean Kaplan, and this is my husband, Harvey," the woman said, smiling up at them.

"I saw you today coming out of your room with another couple," Frank said as he and Joe sat down in the easy chairs opposite the sofa. "I think they're developers—Daniel Doherty and Susan Howell."

"Oh, you've heard of them," Harvey Kaplan said. "They've just sold us a beautiful condo in a brand-new retirement village near here. Got a great price for it, too."

"Dan and Sue told us that our grandchildren will love visiting us with the Fourth Dimension so close by," Mrs. Kaplan said, smiling. "That convinced me."

Frank leaned forward and spoke quietly. "Mr. Kaplan, we have reason to believe these developers are really scam artists."

"They didn't sell you a condo," Joe put in. "They sold you a worthless piece of real estate."

The Kaplans stared at Frank and Joe for a moment, then burst out laughing.

"What imaginations you young people have," Jean Kaplan said, shaking her head. "Why, Dan and Sue's credentials were excellent. We were lucky to get in on such a good deal."

"In fact, if we hadn't seen the Fourth Dimension's terrific ad in *Golden Years* magazine," Harvey Kaplan added, "we would never have come down here to meet Dan and Sue."

"What did the magazine ad say?" Frank asked the Kaplans.

"Well, it was a personal invitation to seniors from Andrew Taylor, the park's owner, to spend time here," Mrs. Kaplan said. "The ad listed special rates at the hotel, so we decided to come here instead of Florida."

"We'd better get going, hon," Mr. Kaplan said

quickly. "We've still got packing to do. We're leaving tomorrow," he explained.

After the Kaplans had left, Frank said, "You know, I'm beginning to wonder if Andrew Taylor might be involved in this case."

"I see what you mean," Joe said. "It seems kind of fishy that he's trying to get retirees to come down here. Maybe he's setting them up as pigeons for the scammers."

"Let's get up really early tomorrow and do some investigating," Frank suggested. "I want to search the offices of Taylor, Maceda, and Kramer. And I need to do it before they show up for work."

"I'll check out the Space Flight Building," Joe said. "It's one of the buildings Dad circled, and it's next to the Command Center. I just hope that this time we find some clues that will lead us to Dad."

Frank nodded but didn't say anything. He didn't want to admit it, but deep down he was worried. They had been investigating for two days. Were Fenton Hardy's kidnappers too clever for them? Would Frank and Joe be able to save their father's life? Frank knew he should call his mother and aunt, but he couldn't bring himself to give them the bad news—he still had no idea where his father was.

At six o'clock the next morning, the Hardys, dressed in their interns' uniforms, left their room and headed for the fire stairs. It was Joe's idea to avoid the lobby.

"If Strauss is on duty and sees us, he might get suspicious," he told Frank.

The brothers entered the park through the arch in the concrete wall Joe had seen the day before. The monorail wasn't running yet, so they crossed the deserted, dimly lit park on foot.

As they approached the Command Center, they spotted a security guard unlocking the door to the building.

"Aren't you guys a little early for work?" the guard asked them with a smile.

"Mr. Maceda asked me to get some material for the Sci-Fi Exhibit from his office," Frank lied. "And my brother needs to take down some photos in the Space Flight Building."

"We wanted to get our errands over early, before we have to show up for our daily assignments," Joe added.

"Well, the Space Flight Building is open," the guard said, after glancing at their ID badges. "But you'll need a key to get into Mr. Maceda's office." He unhooked a key from the ring attached to his belt and handed it to Frank. "This key is a master to all three offices in the Command Center. Return it to security when you're finished with it, okay?"

"No problem," Frank replied. The guard turned and strolled away.

"It's six-thirty," Joe said. "Let's plan to meet back here in an hour."

"Right," Frank said. Then he jogged off toward the Command Center.

Joe turned and headed for the huge geodesic dome that housed the Space Flight Building. When he got there, he stepped into the building and glanced around.

The room was decorated with spacecraft replicas and science-fiction comic book characters. Some spacecraft had been built to scale, while others were smaller models. In the middle of the floor was a twelve-foot tall replica of a United States space shuttle standing upright in the takeoff position. Attached to the replica were metal struts. Joe figured they were part of the mechanism that moved the replica in different positions to simulate flight. He noticed that ventilation grates were set into the floor.

Joe began to search each spacecraft carefully. But after searching for half an hour, he hadn't found a single clue.

He'd left the space shuttle for last. As he approached it, he saw that a chain had been placed around the replica. A sign hanging from the chain said Simulator Opening Soon. Stepping over the chain, Joe climbed the stairs leading to the entrance, slid open the door, and walked into the spacecraft. He sat down in one of the astronaut's chairs and examined the control board that circled the small capsule. It was equipped with countless dials, switches, and meters.

All of a sudden, he heard the door slam shut. The lights on the ceiling flashed on, and a voice said, "Welcome aboard, astronauts. Fasten your seat belts and prepare for lift-off." Then the voice began a countdown.

Joe rushed to the door and tried to pull it open, but it wouldn't budge. He began to feel the capsule vibrate as the voice said, "Three . . . two . . . one." There was a roaring sound. Joe glanced at the video screen in front of the chair he had been sitting in and saw the earth dropping away with frightening speed. The capsule began to vibrate more and more violently.

As Joe grappled his way toward the seats, the spacecraft suddenly turned on its side. Joe fell backward onto the control panel. His head hit something hard, then everything went black.

10 A Rough Flight

Frank searched through a pile of papers on top of Andrew Taylor's desk. Being in the theme park owner's office was making him very nervous.

Suddenly, a computer printout titled "Golden Years" caught Frank's eye. He pulled the printout from the pile and scanned the list of names, noting that many of them had single or double check marks next to them. About halfway down the list he saw Ernest Brody's name, with a single check next to it. Frank flipped through the pages of the printout until he found the names he was looking for—Jean and Harvey Kaplan. Next to the Kaplans' names were two checks.

Frank bit his lip thoughtfully. Had Taylor made the single check marks to show who had been approached by the scam artists? he wondered. Did the double checks indicate people who had bought condos?

Frank glanced at his watch and saw that it was nearly seven. He knew that Maceda got to his office around seven-thirty. It was very possible that Laurel Kramer arrived at the Command Center at the same time as her boss. He was going to have to work faster if he wanted to finish in time.

Shoving the printout back under the pile of papers, he flicked off the desk lamp and left the office. He hurried over to Maceda's office and inserted the key in the lock. To his surprise, the key wouldn't turn.

He must have changed the lock, Frank thought. But maybe the connecting door in Kramer's office is open. He moved over to Laurel's office and tried the key. This time it worked.

Frank entered the office, shut the door, and turned on the light. In the room was a desk, chair, and filing cabinet against the back wall. The only objects on Laurel's desk were a computer, printer, and cordless phone. The desk itself was a table with no drawers.

Frank stepped over to the filing cabinet and opened the bottom drawer. He reached into the drawer and pulled out a small white folder lying underneath a pair of sneakers. He opened the folder and found a dark blue bankbook tucked inside the flap. Printed on the cover was the name of a bank in Georgia. An account number was printed on the inside cover under the name Sara Smith. Frank saw that large sums of money had been deposited in the account every week for the past month and a half, adding up to a balance of over fifty thousand dollars.

Unless Laurel Kramer is holding on to someone else's bankbook, Frank thought, this could be some of the scam victims' money deposited by her under an alias. But he realized he had to come up with some proof that the name was really an alias and that the bankbook belonged to Laurel.

He replaced the bankbook in the filing cabinet, went over to the connecting door, and turned the knob. The door opened, and Frank stepped into Justin Maceda's office. He flicked on the light switch and looked around. He noticed that on top of Maceda's desk were two blueprints. When Frank went over and picked up the blueprints, he saw that one of them was a drawing of a robot. On the other blueprint was the design for a video game called Escape from the Labyrinth.

Just then, the computer next to Frank began to let out a series of loud beeps. He looked at the computer and saw the words *Malfunction, SS Sim. Vibration Approaching Max. Rider Inside* flashing on the screen.

"Space Shuttle Simulator?" Frank said, frowning. "That's in the Space Flight Building." Then it suddenly hit him. "Oh, no! Joe might be in there!"

Still clutching the blueprints, Frank started for the door that led into the other office. At the same moment, he heard a key turn in the lock. The door opened and Frank almost collided with Justin Maceda.

Maceda's expression changed from surprise to anger when he saw the blueprints in Frank's hand. "Give me those," he snapped, grabbing the blueprints from Frank. "No one is supposed to see them."

Then he turned sharply toward the computer. "What's wrong?" he demanded. "Why is it beeping?"

"You've got to stop the simulator!" Frank cried. "I think Joe's in there!"

Maceda hurried over to the computer and began to type in some commands. "It's the door sensor," he muttered as he typed. "A glitch in it causes the door to shut automatically when someone enters the shuttle, activating the ride. If no one is programming the ride, it goes out of control."

The beeping suddenly stopped. "The vibration has ended. The shuttle is back in the upright position," Maceda said. He reached for the phone. "I'd better call the park's emergency medical team."

Frank nodded and hurried out the door. He ran out of the Command Center and over to the Space Flight Building. Once inside, he rushed over to the space shuttle, leaped over the chain, and raced up the stairs.

"Joe!" he shouted as he yanked open the door.

He gasped as his brother's unconscious body fell backward out of the shuttle.

Frank caught Joe in his arms, unsure of whether he should try to get his brother down the stairs or wait for the emergency squad. He had had some first-aid training, but he didn't know what kind of injuries Joe might have after being tossed around violently in the vibrating simulator. If Joe was badly hurt, moving him could make his injuries worse.

Suddenly he heard the sounds of footsteps coming toward the shuttle. He looked down and saw two paramedics hurrying across the floor with a gurney. Maceda and two security guards followed close behind them.

"Don't move him," one of the paramedics called to Frank. "We're coming up."

When the paramedics reached Frank, one of them gently lifted Joe out of Frank's arms. Frank went down the stairs and watched as the paramedics carried Joe to the gurney.

"How is he?" Frank asked anxiously after one of the paramedics had examined his brother.

"No broken bones or internal injuries," the woman told him. "Just some bumps and bruises. But he should probably stay in bed for the rest of the day. He may have a concussion."

Just then, Joe came to with a groan. His eyes blinked open, and he gazed up at his brother.

"You're going to be okay," Frank told him gently. "You just need some rest."

Joe closed his eyes again. "I feel like I just went for a ride in a blender," he said weakly.

The paramedics wheeled Joe out of the room. There wasn't room for Frank in the park's mini-ambulance, but he told Joe he'd see him back at the hotel shortly.

After the ambulance had driven away, Frank saw Maceda coming toward him.

"I'm sorry for my rude behavior back at the office," Maceda said. "And I want to explain why I became upset when I saw you with those blueprints."

Frank nodded. "I'm listening."

"I was afraid Andrew Taylor might see them," Maceda told him. "He would accuse me of wasting time on new designs, as he always does. You see, I decided to try to recreate and modify the designs that were stolen, in case the originals are never recovered." Maceda paused for a moment and frowned. "By the way, what were you doing in my office so early in the morning?" he asked.

"I was looking for clues that might help identify the thief," Frank said, thinking fast. "And Joe had an idea that the thief might have hidden the blueprints in one of the spacecraft. I didn't find anything. And you saw what happened to my brother."

"Yes," Maceda said with a sigh. "An unfortunate accident. Well, I really must go back to my office and try to reprogram that simulator."

Was Joe's wild ride in the simulator an accident,

as Maceda claimed? Frank wondered. He watched the architect hurry off in the direction of the Command Center. Or had someone, possibly Maceda himself, programmed it to go out of control? And could Maceda be lying about the blueprints Frank had found?

"Too many questions and not enough answers," Frank muttered. He turned and headed for the monorail, which was running again.

But the biggest question of all still remains, Frank thought as he boarded the train. He sat down and stared out the window at the gleaming buildings of the Fourth Dimension. In which one had the kidnappers hidden their father?

When Frank got back to the hotel room, he found Joe lying in bed, munching on a piece of toast. There was a room service cart next to his bed.

Frank took a piece of bacon off one of the plates on the cart. "I guess you're okay if you have an appetite for breakfast."

"A little groggy, but that's about it," Joe replied. "I want to hear what happened in the Command Center while my brains were being whipped into a milk shake."

Frank sat on the edge of the bed and told his brother about the list of names, the bankbook, and the blueprints he'd found in Taylor's office.

"Any one of the suspects could have taken Taylor's list and photocopied it," Frank said. "But I still think Taylor is a suspect. He could be running

91

the scam operation with Kramer and Strauss. But how does Maceda fit in?"

"I don't know," Joe said. He sat up and began to pull on his black canvas boots. "But right now I want to forget about untangling all these suspects and continue searching for Dad."

Frank shook his head. "No way, Joe. You're supposed to be resting, remember?"

"I'm rested," Joe said impatiently. "I feel fine now. So let's pick one of the buildings Dad circled on the map and get over there, okay?" He pulled the map out of his pocket and studied it intently. "How about the Hall of Holograms?"

"Okay," Frank said reluctantly as he stood up from the bed. "But if you start feeling dizzy, we're coming right back here. Agreed?"

Joe glared at him. "I really hate it when you play big brother, you know that?"

"Hey," Frank said with a grin as they left the room, "it's a tough job, but someone's got to do it."

"Oh, give me a break," Joe muttered, rolling his eyes.

"Let's walk instead of riding the monorail," Joe said as they left the hotel. "I feel like stretching my legs."

"Fine with me," Frank replied.

The brothers set off to walk through the park. As they passed the theater, Joe nudged his brother. "Isn't that Brody walking about ten feet ahead of us?" he asked.

"Yeah," Frank said, squinting. "But why is he walking with that guy in an alien costume?"

"Let's get a closer look at them," Joe said.

The Hardys began to walk faster. Soon they were close enough to Brody to see that his companion was dressed in the same scaly-looking armor, rubber claws, and one-eyed mask worn by Mike Strauss.

Then Frank saw that one of the alien's hands was shoved up against Brody's ribs. "Joe!" Frank whispered. "I think he's holding a gun to Brody."

Brody and the man in the alien costume began to walk more quickly. Frank and Joe followed at a safe distance.

"We've got to get Brody away from him," Joe said desperately. "But we also have to keep that guy from firing his gun."

Brody and the man suddenly made a sharp left turn toward the roller coaster entrance. Frank saw the man shove Brody into the first car. The ride began to move.

"Come on," Joe shouted to Frank. The two of them ran toward the roller coaster and jumped into the sixth and last car.

The Hardys sat down and buckled their seat belts just in time. The roller coaster shot through a tunnel and began to pick up speed as it approached the first incline.

"I just thought of something," Joe said suddenly. "What if the guy's planning to shoot Brody in one of these tunnels?" He unbuckled his seat belt and stood up.

"What are you doing?" Frank asked harshly.

"I'm going after the guy," Joe said as he began to crawl out the front of the car.

The next car was empty. First Joe had to climb over the nose of the car he was in. Then he grabbed the back of the seat and pulled himself in the car ahead of him. He stood up just as the roller coaster came to another tunnel at the top of an incline. There was a split-second pause before the ride began to barrel down a steep decline. The sudden lurch of the roller coaster heading into the dark tunnel made Joe lose his balance.

Joe lost all sense of direction as the ride went one way and he went the other. Blindly groping for a handhold, he began to fall backward into dark, empty space.

11 The Masked Alien

Joe managed to twist his body so that he was sliding toward the front of the car. He flattened himself on it, then grabbed the back of the car in front of him. Climbing into the seat, he ended up between a man and a boy just as the roller coaster finished its descent and the track straightened.

"Hey, what do you think you're doing?" the man shouted angrily.

"Relax and enjoy the ride," Joe said as he made his way into the next car.

The car was empty. Joe stood up and was about to move on when the roller coaster plunged downward into a tunnel. Suddenly, Joe noticed jagged white objects appearing overhead in the distance, and for a moment he thought the roller coaster would collide with them. As the objects flashed by, he saw that they were simply holograms of asteroids.

The roller coaster shot out of the tunnel, and Joe saw the masked alien and Brody two cars ahead. It was a relief to see that Brody looked unhurt.

Just then, the roller coaster made a sharp left turn. Joe's right elbow banged into the side of the car. "Ow," he yelled before he could stop himself.

The man in the alien costume jerked his head around. Then he stood up and began to crawl over the back of his car toward Joe. Just as the man reached the inside of the second car, the roller coaster lurched to the right. He grabbed the back of the car to steady himself, and Joe glimpsed a red watch with a black, star-shaped dial on the man's left wrist. The man didn't seem to be carrying a gun.

Just then Frank slid into the car next to him and said, "We've got company, Joe." The masked alien entered the car and lunged at Joe. One of the man's claws tightened around Joe's neck.

Joe managed to choke out, "Frank . . . help!" Frank hurled himself forward and pushed hard against the alien's chest. "Get off him!" Frank growled. The alien's grip on Joe loosened.

Suddenly, the roller coaster entered a cavern. The ceiling was decorated to look like the night sky. Joe felt a fist slam hard into his stomach. Breathless, he clutched his stomach and sank to the seat of the car.

He looked up in time to see the masked alien

elbow Frank in the stomach. "Hold on, Frank!" Joe cried out.

Frank staggered backward. He'd lost his balance and was about to fall off the speeding roller coaster!

Joe jumped up and grabbed Frank just as he was about to fall over the edge.

The roller coaster exited the cavern into the blinding sunlight. Joe turned and saw the masked alien crawling toward the last car of the roller coaster. Joe was about to go after him, when he felt Frank grab his arm.

"Sit down. Look at that," Frank shouted, pointing straight ahead.

Joe turned and saw that the track ahead looped up and around in a complete circle. He quickly sat down next to Frank and buckled his seat belt. Seconds later, the roller coaster went up and around the circle, so that Frank and Joe were momentarily upside down. Then the ride made another series of turns and descents.

The Hardys stayed seated until the ride ended. As soon as the roller coaster stopped, the brothers and Brody unbuckled their seat belts and stepped out of their cars. All of them were a little wobbly on their legs.

"Are you okay?" Joe asked the older man.

Brody nodded. "I'm a little shaky, though."

"I don't see the alien," Frank said in a perplexed tone as he watched the two other passengers get off the roller coaster. Frank hurried after the man and boy as they started to leave the ride.

"Excuse me," he said to them. "Did you see someone wearing an alien costume get off the roller coaster?"

"Yeah," the man said. "He jumped off when we were riding that open stretch about five feet from the ground."

Frank returned to Joe and Brody and told them what the man had said.

"I can't believe we let him get away," Joe said.

Frank turned to Brody. "Tell us what happened," he urged.

"I'd just started to walk through the park to see if I could spot the scam artists," Brody explained. "Suddenly, the alien grabbed my arm and stuck a gun in my ribs. At least I thought it was a gun." He reached into his pants pocket and pulled out a short, thick stick of wood. "He used this to fool me into thinking he had a gun. He dropped it on the floor when he saw you, Joe."

"Did he say anything when he grabbed you?" Joe asked.

"He said to come with him quietly and I wouldn't get hurt," Brody replied. "He also said he was going to put me 'down there for a while' with his 'other friend.' I assume he meant your father. I think he saw you following us, because he muttered something about making a slight detour. Then he shoved me onto the roller coaster. I don't think he expected you to follow us onto the ride."

"I didn't notice anything about that guy that

might help us identify him," Frank said. "Did either of you?"

"His voice was kind of raspy," Brody said.

"Like the voice of the guy who warned us on the phone in Maceda's office," Frank murmured. He turned to his brother. "Joe?"

Joe thought a minute. "I think he was wearing a red watch with a black, star-shaped dial."

Frank's eyes opened wide. "You know who wears a watch like that? Steve Willis."

"But how do we know that Strauss or some other staffer doesn't have a watch like Willis's?" Joe pointed out.

"Strauss's watch is black and looks like mine," Frank said. "I noticed it when we checked in. You might be right about other staffers wearing the same watch as Willis, but I think we should check him out, anyway."

"Why don't we ask Mark Hoffman, the guy who was in charge of the gladiator game?" Joe suggested. "He might know something about Willis and the watch."

Frank nodded. "Let's call him from the hotel. Maybe we can reach him at the arena."

When they got back to the hotel, the Hardys saw that Strauss had left the reception desk. The card reading Please call Room 1506 for Manager was back in place.

"Think he's up there planning the next scam operation?" Joe asked. Then he turned to Brody. "Mr. Brody, you should—" he began.

"I know what you're going to say," Brody interrupted. "You think that this time I should take your advice and leave the Fourth Dimension." He shook his head. "I'm not going anywhere and that's final."

"Well, don't do any more investigating, okay?" Frank said. "We may not be around the next time the kidnappers go after you."

"Just stay in your room with the door double locked," Joe advised. "And be extra careful when you're coming back and forth from the restaurant."

"All right," Brody said meekly. "I'll do whatever you say."

The three of them got onto the elevator. As they were riding up to Brody's floor, Frank suddenly turned to the older man. "Do you happen to remember the name of the construction company that's supposed to be working at that site?"

"Let me see," Brody said slowly. "Oh, yes, I do remember. It was on the trailer. D. S. Burt Construction."

Frank nodded. "I thought it might be a good idea to find out who's really developing that site," he said. "It's a long shot, but they just might be connected to the case."

After Brody had gotten off the elevator, the Hardys continued on to the fifteenth floor. As soon as they stepped off the elevator into the hallway, they saw a man in a staff uniform come out of room 1506.

"I'll be back to pick up my tax return in a week,"

he called over his shoulder. "I hope you can get me a refund, Mike." The man walked toward the elevator.

Frank and Joe looked at each other. " 'Tax return? Refund?' " Joe said softly.

"Excuse me," Frank said to the man who had just left Room 1506. "Are you having your taxes prepared by Mike Strauss?"

"That's right," the man replied. "He was an accountant before he decided to go into hotel management. He prepares tax returns for a lot of the staffers here. His fee is very reasonable," he added as he got on the elevator.

The other elevator arrived. After the brothers had stepped inside, Joe asked, "Do you think Strauss is trying to pay back money he stole from the Chicago hotel by preparing tax returns?"

"It's possible," Frank said. "But he owes a lot of money. He might still be running the scam operation. We need more proof before we cross him off our list of suspects."

The elevator stopped on the ninth floor, and the Hardys got out. As soon as they entered their room, Frank headed over to the phone. He dialed the arena and asked for Mark Hoffman. After a few moments, he heard a voice say, "This is Mark Hoffman."

Frank identified himself, then asked Mark if he knew Steve Willis.

"Yeah, I know him," Mark replied. "He works

here off and on. I've used him for the Space War Gladiator Game, and sometimes he demonstrates the hovercraft cars."

"Do you know how I can get in touch with him?" Frank asked.

"Sorry, I don't," Mark said. "Steve doesn't mingle with the other staffers, and no one, except Justin, knows where he lives. Justin's got every staffer's personnel file. Anything else I can tell you?"

Frank asked Mark about the red watch with the star-shaped dial.

"Yeah, a lot of staffers wear them," Mark said. "Heather Baker has a bunch of them down in the costume room. They come in different colors. If you want one, just ask her."

Frank thanked Mark for the information and hung up. Then he told his brother what Mark had said.

"Well, we can't ask Maceda about Willis," Joe said with a sigh. "We'll just have to be on the lookout for him." He pulled the phone book out of the drawer and looked up D. S. Burt Construction. He found the number and dialed it. Joe spoke to the person who answered the call for a few minutes, then he hung up and turned to his brother.

"The developer of the construction site is none other than Andrew Taylor," he announced.

"Well, that's very interesting," Frank said. "I think we should have another look in Taylor's office.

I didn't have time to give it a thorough search this morning. There may be some clues I missed."

"Okay, but let's wait until after dinner," Joe said. "I'd rather search Taylor's office when he's not there."

Frank smiled. "Good thinking."

When the brothers arrived at the Command Center after dinner, they were relieved to find that the building was still open. They stepped inside and saw that the only person in the building was a lone programmer sitting at a work station.

"We just need to get some materials from Mr. Taylor's office," Joe told him. The young man nodded and turned back to his computer.

Frank and Joe went over to Taylor's office. Frank tried the door, but it was locked.

"Now what do we do?" Joe asked. "I doubt if that programmer has a key."

"No problem," Frank said with a grin. He reached into his pocket and pulled out a key. "This is the master key the guard gave me this morning, remember? I never returned it to security."

Once he and Joe were inside the office, they split up. Frank began to search the bookcase; Joe concentrated on a wooden filing cabinet in the corner behind the desk.

"Look at this, Frank," Joe said about ten minutes later. He had pulled an unmarked folder out of the bottom drawer and was examining the contents.

Frank went over to his brother. "What is it?"

Joe took a thin piece of white cardboard out of the folder and lifted up the sheet of tissue paper that was attached to it.

"It's a design of a *Golden Years* magazine ad for the Fourth Dimension," he said.

"'Spend your golden years with us,'" Frank read. He looked at his brother. "That ad makes it sound like Taylor is inviting people to come and retire here. He could be the guy who's setting them up for the scam."

"Just what do you think you're doing?"

The Hardys turned quickly and saw Andrew Taylor standing by the door, his face twisted with rage.

The silver-haired man put a hand in his jacket pocket and began to move menacingly toward Frank and Joe.

"You won't get away with this," he snarled. "I'll teach you to go nosing around my office!"

"He's got a gun," Joe whispered to his brother as Taylor moved toward them.

Oh, no, Frank thought as he felt his body tense. How are we going to get out of this one?

12 Caught in the Act

Before the Hardys could make a move, Taylor pulled his hand out of his pocket. Instead of the gun Frank and Joe were expecting, Taylor held a cordless phone in his hand. Frank and Joe exchanged a relieved glance.

"I'm going to call security and have you thrown out of the park immediately," Taylor announced. "Oh, and by the way, you're both fired." He began to punch numbers into the phone.

"That won't stop us from informing the police about the scam operation you're running here," Joe said boldly. "Or the fact that you've kidnapped our father."

Taylor pressed the Off button and stared at Joe.

"What are you talking about?" he demanded. "What scam operation? What kidnapping?"

"Oh, come on, Mr. Taylor," Frank said, pointing to the *Golden Years* ad. "We know you use this ad to lure retirees here. Then you have a phony developer sell them nonexistent condos on commercially zoned land. Land that's owned by *you*. I even saw a printout with the checked-off names of your victims."

"You found out that our father was a private detective hired to uncover the operation," Joe added angrily. "So you had him kidnapped."

"This is ridiculous," Taylor snapped. "I haven't kidnapped anyone. And of course I try to get retirees down here—they have the time to travel. I cut a fly/drive deal with a national airline. I advertise special summer rates for families later in the spring. I also place ads in magazines other than *Golden Years*."

He moved over to the file cabinet and pulled out another unmarked folder. "If you look at these ads," he said, handing the file to Joe, "you'll see they've been placed in magazines that aren't especially targeted for seniors."

"What about the printout with the list of names on it?" Frank asked, looking up from the file. "And the commercially zoned construction site?"

Taylor wrung his hands in exasperation. "That checked-off list of people you found happens to be a record of guests who received personalized cards in their rooms that asked them to rate the hotel and the park. One check means that the person or couple received a card. Two checks indicate a response.

"As for the construction site," he continued, "it's a planned extension of the Fourth Dimension—a Space Needle with a revolving restaurant. Justin Maceda keeps telling me his designs for the restaurant aren't quite ready, so construction has been delayed. If you don't believe me, call D. S. Burt Construction."

Frank said slowly, "I think he's telling the truth, Joe."

Taylor glared at them. "Perhaps now you'll be good enough to tell me why I should believe your preposterous story about a scam operation and kidnapping!"

"The scam victim who hired our father is staying in the hotel," Joe told him. "His name is Ernest Brody. You can ask him about the operation."

"Lieutenant Con Riley of the Bayport police force will vouch for us and our dad," Frank added.

Taylor looked at them thoughtfully for a moment. "All right," he said finally. "I'll make these phone calls. I can't afford to dismiss your story completely at this point. I'll contact you in your room later when I've spoken to these people." He sat down at his desk and picked up his reading glasses. "That's all," he said abruptly.

The Hardys headed back to the hotel to wait for

Taylor's call. When they got to their room, they found a folded-up piece of paper shoved under the door.

"It's a computer printout," Frank said as they picked up the paper and read it. Silently he handed the printout to his brother.

" 'Time is running out for your father,' " Joe read aloud. " 'I warned you not to interfere.' " Joe looked at his brother, his eyes wide. "This sounds like the kidnappers are planning to kill Dad!"

"I know," Frank said grimly. "The question is, can we find him first?"

"We're not going to find him if we just sit around here waiting for Taylor to call," Joe said desperately. "Who cares if he believes our story?"

Just then, the phone rang. Frank hurried over to the night table and picked up the receiver. "Frank Hardy here."

"This is Andrew Taylor," the theme park owner announced stiffly. "I spoke to Mr. Brody, who gave me some details of the scam operation you described. I have no reason to doubt his story."

"Did you get hold of Con Riley?" Frank asked.

"I've just gotten off the phone with him," Taylor replied. "According to Lieutenant Riley, you're not in the habit of making up stories. In fact, he praised you and your father as fine detectives. He was also quite concerned about the fate of Fenton Hardy. I've decided to do as he suggested and call in the police."

"Please don't contact them yet," Frank said

quickly. He told Taylor about the message on the printout. "The kidnappers might get desperate and decide to kill Dad before the police can get to him. We've already been investigating. We have the best chance of finding him before the kidnappers carry out their threat."

There was silence at the other end of the line. Then Taylor said, "All right. I'll give you twenty-four hours. After that, I call the police. I want those criminals caught. I'm fed up with what's going on at my park. First there was the computer theft, then the hotel safe was robbed. It's a disgrace."

"So Strauss told you about the theft?" Frank asked.

"Yes, he did tell me," Taylor replied. "He also confessed that he had committed a theft at his last job, but that he was paying back the money."

"Thanks for letting us know that," Frank said. "There's just one more thing. Can you get us keys to the buildings here? We need to start searching them now, and they probably won't be open. It's after ten." He listened to Taylor's response, then hung up.

Frank told his brother what Taylor had said. "I think we can take Strauss off the suspect list now," he added.

Joe nodded. "He wouldn't have confessed everything to Taylor if he was running a scam operation."

"Taylor also told me we can pick up a master key that opens all the buildings at the security center. Let's get over there." Frank started for the door.

"Wait a minute," Joe said, heading over to his suitcase. He reached inside and pulled out a flashlight. "The single most important tool for searching dark buildings," he said with a grin.

After the brothers left the security center, Joe said, "Okay, which building do we head for first?"

"I've been thinking about that," Frank replied. "Brody's would-be kidnapper said he was going to take Brody 'down there,' remember?"

Joe's eyes lit up. "What if there's a basement or underground storeroom in one of these buildings? That's where they could be holding Dad!"

"Right," Frank said. "And maybe, just maybe, that's where the red-haired guy went when he disappeared down that mini-elevator."

The brothers turned east and walked over to the building housing the Science-Fiction Exhibit. Joe unlocked the door and they stepped inside.

Frank took the flashlight from his brother. "This way," he said, heading for the flight of stairs.

He tried the door at the top of the stairs. "Oh, right," he said with a sigh. "I forgot that this door is locked." He tried the master key, but it didn't work.

"Let me see what I can do," Joe said, pulling his Swiss army knife out of his pocket. He plucked out a tiny screwdriver and began to pick the lock.

After a few moments, there was a click. Joe turned the knob and opened the door.

"Nice work," Frank said. He led the way across the room over to the red curtain. "Here it is," he said, pulling the curtain aside.

"How does it work?" Joe asked, frowning at the semicircular glass capsule.

"Stand on that metal disk in the middle of the platform," Frank told him, aiming the flashlight at the floor of the capsule. "Press one of those buttons on the control panel. I hope that one of the buttons will take the elevator down like last time."

Frank watched as Joe stood on the disk and, hesitating for just a moment, pressed a button. Immediately, his brother disappeared in a puff of smoke.

When the smoke cleared, Frank saw that the disk was back in place. He stepped onto it, pressed the button, and felt himself being whisked straight downward. Seconds later, the elevator slowed to a stop. He turned and stepped off the disk onto a concrete floor.

There was a gentle whine as the elevator shot upward again. Frank saw a control panel near the elevator and figured the red-haired man must have deactivated the elevator when Frank tried to use it last time.

"Shine the flashlight around, and let's see where we are," he heard Joe say.

"It looks like some sort of workshop or storage area," Frank observed as he surveyed the room.

"There's a doorway on one side of the room," Joe

noted. "I wonder if this underground area curves around the whole park."

"Well, Dad's not in this room, so there must be other areas," Frank said. "Let's keep walking."

When they entered the next room, Frank shined the flashlight around. "Nothing here but boxes and packing crates. Let's keep going."

The brothers had walked through two more rooms filled with boxes and crates when they heard the sound of footsteps coming toward them.

"Kill the light," Joe whispered quickly. He and Frank crouched down behind a packing crate and listened as the footsteps grew louder. Suddenly, the dark shape of a short man stepped into the room holding a flashlight.

Joe sprang out from behind the crate and pushed the man to the floor. "Where's our father, Maceda?" Joe demanded. "Tell us, or I'll—"

"Stop, Joe, it's me—Ernest Brody!" the man on the floor cried breathlessly. He raised his arm and shined his flashlight on his bearded face. "See?"

Joe got up and helped Brody to his feet. "I'm really sorry, Mr. Brody," he said. "Are you okay?"

"I'm fine," Brody reassured him. "And I can understand why you thought I was Maceda. We're both short, and it's dark in here."

"Mr. Brody, I thought we told you to stay in your room," Frank said in an exasperated tone.

"There was an after-dinner viewing of the night sky in the observatory near the Space Flight Building," Brody told them. "I slipped away to the Space Flight Building to do some investigating. I found a trapdoor under one of the ventilator grates with steps that led down here."

"Did you find any clues between the Space Flight Building and here?" Frank asked. "Something that might lead us to Dad?"

Brody shook his head. "All I saw besides boxes and crates was a bookcase with a rolled-up blueprint on one of the shelves. I couldn't really see very well," he added with an apologetic shrug. "My flashlight isn't very strong, and my eyes aren't what they used to be."

"Let's go take a look at that blueprint," Joe said.

Brody led the Hardys through the underground area to a flight of stone steps that led to a bookcase. When they reached the top of the steps, Joe found the blueprint and unrolled it.

"This is strange," Frank said, frowning. "It looks like a design for a small amusement park." He pointed to a spot on the blueprint. "There's a video arcade with an area marked off for a game called Escape from the Labyrinth. And over here is an information center with a drawing of a robot next to it." He looked at Joe and Brady. "The blueprints Maceda said were stolen were for a robot and the same video game."

"What if he's planning to open his own small-scale, high-tech amusement park?" Joe suggested. "He could be running the scam operation to get the money for it." He rolled up the blueprint and stuck it back in the bookcase. As he did, he felt something soft. He pulled it off the shelf and held it up.

"A long blond wig," Frank said. "I'm willing to bet that it was worn by Laurel Kramer when she posed as the chambermaid."

Brody leaned back against the bookcase. "But how do you know . . ." he started to say. All of a sudden there was a click and the bookcase swung inward.

Joe grabbed Brody's arm to keep him from losing his balance, while Frank shined the flashlight into the dark space beyond. They could see a desk with a computer and telephone on it. On the wall was a framed diploma with a name the Hardys had no trouble recognizing.

"It's Maceda's office," Joe said. "So this is how he and Laurel get down here."

After Frank pushed the bookcase back in place, he and the others headed down the steps and continued through the underground area.

They passed the steps leading up to the Space Flight Building without finding any other clues. About ten minutes later, they came to another set of steps.

"We've reached the next building," Brody said. "The Hall of Holograms. We've been curving northwest around the park."

"Let's keep going," Frank said. "Dad's got to be down here somewhere."

Suddenly they heard the sound of a person moaning in pain.

"Did you hear that, Frank?" Joe asked, grabbing his brother's arm and pointing up the stairs.

Frank nodded, then stood still and listened intently. The door at the top of the steps began to open slowly. Inside the door was a man tied to a chair.

"Dad!" Frank and Joe shouted.

13 A Dirty Trick

Joe raced up the steps, followed by Frank and Brody. He heard the door slam shut behind them, but was too concerned about their father to think much of it.

As the brothers rushed toward their father, Fenton Hardy suddenly began to fade away. There was a hissing sound, and they saw tiny flames crackling around a space to the left of where their father had been. The flames disappeared, and the moaning died down.

Low, menacing laughter filled the room. Then a voice called out softly, "Fooled you again. You'll never find him. Never . . . never . . ."

Frank aimed his flashlight at the ceiling. "There's

a speaker up there," he reported when the laughing voice had faded away.

"But where's Dad?" Joe demanded. "What happened to him?"

"I think what we just saw was a hologram of him," Frank said. He moved forward, shining the flashlight in front of him.

"A what?" Brody asked.

"A hologram is a three-dimensional image of a photograph," Frank explained. "It's made by shining laser light in a certain way through the photo. The lit-up image looks real, but it isn't."

Frank aimed the flashlight at a stand with a charred photographic plate mounted on it. "One of the kidnappers took a photo of Dad. Then he set it up in front of holography equipment and programmed the equipment to switch on. The photo itself was probably wired in some way so that it would burn up." He shook his head. "That was a really horrible trick to play on us."

"It looks like this is Maceda's holography workroom," Joe said, glancing around at the tables and photographic equipment in the large windowless room. "We're at ground level now. The exhibit must be upstairs on the second floor."

Brody tried the door that led to the underground area. "Locked," he said. "Can we break it open?"

Joe took the flashlight from Frank and examined the door. After a moment, he shook his head. "This door has a lock that can only be opened with a

V-shaped key. We'd need a piece of metal that was exactly the same shape and width, and I don't think we're going to find one here."

The Hardys and Brody searched the room and found the unlocked door leading up to the second-floor exhibit. Once upstairs, they moved past more holography equipment and video monitors and exited the building.

"We have to get back into the underground area," Frank said. "Dad's just got to be down there somewhere."

"Let's try to get in at the Home of the Future," Joe suggested. "Maybe Dad circled that building because he found a secret door there." He looked at his watch. "It's almost one A.M., Mr. Brody. Don't you want to go back to the hotel and get some rest?"

Brody shook his head. "I'm not tired, and I want to be there when you find Fenton." He smiled at Frank and Joe. "Believe it or not, I'm enjoying myself. Retirement was getting to be pretty boring."

"I guess we can understand that," Frank said, smiling back at him.

The three of them headed south, past the Video Arcade to the two-story, five-sided, white brick building that housed the Home of the Future. As soon as they stepped inside, they heard a buzzing sound. Then the fluorescent lights on the ceiling flickered on.

The Hardys and Brody saw that they were standing in a small living room that contained a backless sofa, a long piece of glass set into the floor in front of it, and two red leather rockers with curving seats and backs. Off to the right was a kitchen area that included a washer and drier. To the left was a hallway.

Joe flopped down on one of the red rocking chairs and glanced around. "So where do we start looking for the secret door?"

Before Frank could answer, a voice suddenly boomed, "Welcome to the Home of the Future." He looked across the room and saw the smiling face of a woman on a TV screen set in the wall.

"Through the use of infrared motion detectors, your presence has automatically activated this home," said the woman. "By simply touching a selection on this screen, you will be able to program the computer to run any of the devices in this house. Enjoy your stay in the future."

The woman vanished, and a list of appliances and chores appeared in boxes on the screen.

"Too bad we don't have time to try out . . ." Joe began. Suddenly his chair began to rock back and forth violently. Joe laughed and gripped the arms tightly. Then it pitched forward, throwing him onto the floor. As Frank hurried over to help him, the lights on the ceiling began to flicker.

Everything started to happen at once. The piece of glass on the floor rose up on a pedestal and hit Brody, who was standing right near it. He howled in pain and staggered backward onto the sofa. The sofa immediately began to fold out into a bed. Both the dishwasher and clothes washer began to vibrate and overflow, sending water streaming onto the floor and out of the kitchen.

The double doors of the refrigerator opened, and a robot arm at the back picked up oranges and threw them in the Hardys' direction. Then the robot picked up a lemon meringue pie and hurled it at Frank. Before Frank could dodge it, the pie hit him right in the face. A panel in the living room wall slid open and the hose of a vacuum cleaner snaked toward them, blowing dust everywhere.

"I don't believe it," Joe said between coughs. "This house is attacking us!"

Frank wiped the pie from his eyes and moved toward the TV screen to find a Stop command, but another robot arm shot out of a door in the wall. The arm began to spray Frank with foam concentrate from the fire extinguisher it held.

"Let's just get out of here," Joe shouted, heading for the door.

Frank and Brody followed him out of the house. The older man handed Frank a handkerchief. As Frank wiped the pie off his face, he looked down at the foam clinging to his pants and shook his head in disgust. Then he faced his brother and Brody.

"I have a feeling I couldn't have made the house stop going haywire even if I had wanted to," he said. "I think Maceda or Kramer overrode the program to make it go out of control."

"They always seem to know where we are," Joe said. "It's almost as if they've been tracking us. But we've been careful to make sure no one has been following us. How are we being tracked?"

Frank shook his head. "I don't know." He thought for a minute, then said, "Maybe they're tracking us with a computer. But that would mean they'd have to have planted tracking devices on us somehow."

"But where?" Joe asked. "They can't be sewn into our uniforms or placed in our boots. The kidnappers couldn't have known we'd pick these exact uniforms from the costume room."

Frank nodded and looked thoughtfully at his brother. Joe was brushing dust from the vacuum cleaner off his ID badge.

Frank stared at the black metallic badge and his eyes lit up. "Hand me your Swiss army knife," he told his brother.

Puzzled, Joe took the knife out of his pocket and gave it to Frank.

Frank unhooked his own badge, then used the tiny screwdriver to remove two little screws at the back of the badge.

"Here it is," he said, holding up a small chip. "One tracking device. I bet one is hidden in your badge, too, Joe."

Joe nodded. "That must be how Maceda knew I was in the Space Flight Building yesterday. The devices are somehow linked to his computer." He unhooked his badge and handed it to Brody.

"If you take our badges back to our room," he explained to the older man, "Maceda and Kramer

121

will think we've given up and gone home. Then we can continue investigating without their knowing it."

Frank saw the look of disappointment on Brody's face and added quickly, "I know you wanted to investigate, but right now, this is the best way you can help us find Dad."

Brody nodded and held out his hand for Frank's badge. "I understand," he said with a smile. "Good luck. Let me know what happens."

Brody headed off in the direction of the hotel. "Now we can look for a secret door in the Home of the Future without getting decked," Joe said.

When the Hardys reentered the house, they saw that it had stopped malfunctioning. The lights flickered on, and once again, the woman on the TV screen gave her speech and the list appeared. But this time, the house stayed calm.

Frank and Joe began to search for the door that would lead them back to the underground area. They looked in the living room, kitchen, bedrooms, and bathroom, but found nothing. As Frank was feeling around the inside wall of the hall closet, he discovered the outline of a door panel.

"I think I found it," he called to his brother.

Joe hurried over and entered the closet just as Frank located a hole with a knob inside it. Frank turned the knob and heard the sound of a bolt moving. "Got it," he said, pushing the panel open.

Joe switched on the flashlight. Then he and

Frank stepped through the doorway onto a flight of stairs leading down into darkness.

When they reached the bottom of the steps, Joe spotted a lamp hanging from the ceiling. He walked over to it and pulled the chain. The room was flooded with light.

Frank gave a low whistle. "Well, what do you know," he said. "I think we just found the *real* command center at this park."

The Hardys stared at a small printing press set up on a table in the room. Frank went over and picked up a pile of brochures advertising New Dimension Retirement Village from the table.

"Take a look at these," Joe said as he sifted through a box on the floor.

"Business cards and drivers' licenses with the names and photos of the phony developers, Daniel Doherty and Susan Howell. Here's one for Sara Smith, the name on the bankbook you found in Kramer's office."

"Here's a photocopy of Taylor's printout with the list of names," Frank said, turning the pages. "None of the names are checked off. Wait a minute," he added as he looked at the last page of the printout. "Here's something interesting."

"What is it?" Joe asked.

"It's a note written next to the name of Mrs. Martha Cerone," Frank told him. "It gives today's date, then says, 'finalize deal in hotel, nine A.M.'" He looked at Joe. "Are you thinking what I'm thinking?"

Joe nodded. "We might be able to get the police to catch the scam artists in the act of accepting a check from this woman," he said. "It's a good idea, but first we have to find Dad."

Suddenly, Joe spotted a gold-colored object lying on the floor next to a stone pillar. He stepped over to the pillar, reached down, and picked up the object.

"It's a gold watch," Frank said, surprised.

"Not just any gold watch," Joe said, turning the watch over. "It's the watch Mom gave Dad on their last anniversary. See? Here's the inscription."

"'To Fenton, All My Love, Laura,'" Frank read. He looked at his brother. "This means Dad was definitely here. But where is he now?"

"Maybe the kidnappers moved him farther down into the underground area," Joe said hopefully.

The brothers continued on until they reached a flight of steps that led up to a door in the Biosphere. They saw that the underground area ended at a brick wall.

"He's obviously not down here anymore," Frank said wearily. "I say we go back to the hotel and plan our next move."

"I think we're running out of moves, Frank," Joe said glumly.

When the brothers got back to their room, Frank changed out of his foam-stained uniform.

"Let's take a look at that video of the park one more time," he said, tucking a clean black T-shirt into his jeans.

"But we didn't spot any clues in it last time," Joe protested. "What makes you think we'll see anything now that will help us?"

"Got any better ideas?" Frank countered.

Joe was silent. He had to admit that he was totally out of ideas. He sat on the edge of his bed, turning his father's watch over and over in his hands. Why had it been left on the floor down in the underground room? he wondered. Did the kidnappers take it off his father's wrist, or had Fenton somehow worked it off himself and dropped it as a clue?

He glanced up at the TV. The video was showing a group of visitors relaxing on benches near the clock tower. Joe stared at the screen, then down at the watch again. "Frank!" he exclaimed. "I think I know where Dad is!"

14 Scam Time

"Freeze the frame," Joe said quickly. Frank pressed a button on the video remote control.

"Good," Joe said. "Right there."

Joe held up the watch. "What if Dad dropped this as a clue to let us know that he was being taken to the clock tower?"

Frank's eyes lit up. "It's definitely worth a try. Let's go!"

The Hardys rushed out of the room, rode the elevator down to the lobby, and ran out of the hotel. They didn't stop until they reached the black steel clock tower in the middle of the park.

Joe pulled open the door, switched on his flashlight, and shined it onto the winding metal stairs.

"Dad?" he called softly, his voice echoing off the metal walls of the clock tower.

Joe looked at his brother. "What if he's not up there after all?" he asked anxiously.

"He may not have heard you if he's at the top of the tower," Frank said. "And if he's been tied up and gagged, he probably can't answer."

Joe took a deep breath. "Well, there's only one way to find out if he's up there or not," he said, starting up the stairs. Frank followed close behind his brother.

Ten minutes later, they reached the top of the stairs, panting hard. They saw a man sitting on the floor tied to a stair railing, a gag in his mouth.

Joe hurried over and removed the gag.

"What took you so long?" Fenton Hardy said hoarsely, smiling up at his younger son.

"We ran into a couple of glitches," Joe said as he untied his father.

"I knew you'd find me sooner or later." Fenton rubbed his wrists and ankles, then slowly got to his feet.

"Not soon enough, Dad," Frank said, helping him up.

"I know you both did the best you could," Fenton said, stretching to get the circulation back in his arms and legs. "Now we have to think of a way to nail the scam artists. But first of all, did you manage to find out who they are?"

Frank and Joe quickly filled their father in on how the investigation was going.

127

"We'll have to catch the scam artists accepting a check from one of their victims," Fenton said. "Otherwise we don't have any actual proof that there is a scam at all."

"We came up with an idea for how to catch them in the act," Frank said. He told his father about Mrs. Martha Cerone, the name they had found on the list of scam victims in the underground area.

"The scammers are finalizing the condo deal with her in the hotel today," Joe added. "If we can get the police to arrive at the same time, they can bust those crooks."

Fenton nodded. "Good idea."

"So, now that that's settled, let's get out of here," Frank said.

Just then, they heard the faint sound of footsteps coming up the stairs.

"It's one of the kidnappers," Frank whispered.

"He may be bringing me food," Fenton said in a low tone. "I haven't eaten anything since yesterday morning. They probably don't want to risk being spotted so they come here at night."

"I say we jump this person and find out who it is," Joe said between his teeth. "I've been waiting a long time to get my hands on one of the kidnappers."

"I know how you feel, Joe," Frank said. "But if we wait until the police witness the scam, we can get two crooks instead of one. If the other scam artist finds this guy has been nabbed, he might bolt."

128

The footsteps were getting closer.

"You'd better gag me and tie me up again," Fenton said quickly. "Then hide outside that window." He motioned quickly to an open window opposite the clock mechanism. "Hurry!"

The Hardys loosely bound and gagged their father, then climbed out the window and slid down onto the narrow ledge that circled the tower. From there, they clung to the windowsill and peered into the room.

A figure in a black robe and a black star-fighter helmet entered the room. Frank saw that the mystery person carried a gun and a paper shopping bag. A few moments later, the star fighter removed Fenton's gag and fed him two sandwiches from the shopping bag.

After Fenton had eaten, the star fighter gagged him and disappeared down the stairs.

The brothers waited ten minutes, then Frank climbed back into the room. When Frank was inside, Joe inched along the ledge to get closer to the window. Suddenly his foot slipped, and he stumbled. His grip on the windowsill loosened, and he started to slide down the side of the hundred-foot building.

Just as he was about to yell, he felt a hand grab one of his arms and pull him up. He gripped the windowsill with his other hand.

"Got it?" he heard his brother ask.

"Yeah," Joe breathed. With Frank's help, he

lifted himself up and over the windowsill into the room. "Now let's get Dad out of here."

After Frank and Joe had released their father, the three Hardys headed down the stairs and out of the clock tower.

"We'd better move fast," Frank cautioned. "That star fighter may still be in the vicinity. We don't want him to see us."

They walked quickly toward the hotel. The younger Hardys had questions they wanted to ask their father, but they knew it would be better to wait until they were back at the hotel room.

When they entered the room, Fenton headed over to one of the beds and lay down on it with a contented sigh. He placed his arm back under his head and turned to face his sons.

"I have a feeling you've got some questions for me," he said, his eyes twinkling in his pale face.

Frank smiled at his father. "You know we do, Dad. But why don't you get some sleep first?"

Fenton shook his head. "I'll answer your questions first. Then I'll sleep."

"What happened the night you were kidnapped?" Frank asked.

"That day I found a fourth secret door leading to the underground area," Fenton explained. "It was in the hall closet in the Home of the Future. I found the printing press, brochures, and phony IDs, but I had no idea who could be using them. I never had the chance to see the scam artists at work.

"I called you because I needed your help in

130

spotting the scammers and identifying them," he continued. "But it seems that one of the scammers spotted *me*—probably entering the secret door to the Home of the Future.

That night, I lay down on my bed to think up a strategy for the investigation and fell asleep, still dressed. The next thing I knew, someone was grabbing me. I woke up and started to struggle, but a cloth soaked with chloroform was pressed to my face. I blacked out. When I came to, I was tied to a pillar in the room under the Home of the Future."

He gave a huge yawn. "I was moved when the scammers knew you two were looking for me. But I was sure you would find me eventually," he said drowsily. His eyes began to close.

"Dad?" Joe called softly. But his father had fallen fast asleep. Joe and Frank moved away from the bed so they wouldn't disturb their father.

"The sooner we call the police and catch these crooks, the better," Frank said in a low tone. "We can't be one hundred percent sure the kidnappers won't pay Dad another surprise visit in the clock tower today."

"Right," Joe said. "If they find out he's gone, they'll probably bolt. But before they do, they could figure out where he is and decide to come after us. They might think that's the only way to make absolutely sure we can't identify them."

"Let's call the police from Brody's room so we don't disturb Dad," Frank suggested.

"I think I should stay up here with him, just in

case the kidnappers do decide to show up," Joe said, glancing at his sleeping father.

Frank nodded, then left the room. He headed down to the fifth floor and knocked on Ernest Brody's door.

"Who is it?" he heard Brody ask uncertainly.

"It's Frank Hardy," Frank said in a low voice. "Can I come in? I need to use your phone."

The door opened, and Brody stood in front of Frank, dressed in a bathrobe over red-striped pajamas. He squinted at Frank in the sudden brightness. "What's going on?" he asked as Frank stepped past him into the room.

Frank explained what had happened after Brody had left them outside the Home of the Future.

"I'm so glad Fenton is safe and sound at last," Brody said with a sigh of relief. Then he listened as Frank told him about how he planned to catch the scam artists.

When Frank had finished, he moved over to the phone and picked up the receiver. He started to dial the number of the local police department, then changed his mind and looked up Andrew Taylor's home phone number in the directory. He found it and punched it into the phone.

After several rings, an irritable voice answered, "Taylor here. Whoever you are, I hope you have a good reason for calling me at five A.M."

"This is Frank Hardy," Frank said, rolling his eyes. "I called to tell you that we've found our

132

father. He's in our room at the hotel, and he's okay. But we need you to help us catch the scam artists."

"What do you want me to do?" Taylor asked, sounding a bit more reasonable.

"We discovered that a victim is making a payment to the scam artists at the hotel today at nine A.M.," Frank told him. "Would you call the local police chief and ask him to send an officer over here to witness it?"

Taylor consented.

"There's just one more thing," Frank added. "Can you find a reason to keep Justin Maceda with you in your office until the police or I call and tell you the scammers have been caught?"

"Yes, yes, but what does that fool Maceda have to do with the scam operation?" Taylor asked.

"We think he's been running the operation," Frank told him. "I don't want to take the chance that he might try to contact the scam artists. If he finds out they've been caught, he might decide to escape before the police can nail him."

"I'll do as you ask," Taylor said. "I'll call you in your room after I've contacted the police."

Frank thanked him and hung up. Then he told Brody what Taylor had said. "I'd better head upstairs to wait for Taylor to call back," he added. "Why don't I call you when the police get here? I'm sure they'll want to talk to you."

"I'll be here," Brody said with a smile.

When Frank returned to the Hardys' room, he

saw that his father was sitting up in bed, sipping a cup of coffee. Joe was sitting next to him.

Frank told his father and brother about his conversation with Andrew Taylor.

"I called Mike Strauss and filled him in on the situation," Fenton reported. "He said he'd let us know as soon as the police arrive. He'll also keep an eye out for Mrs. Cerone."

Just then, the phone rang. Frank picked up the receiver. "This is Frank Hardy," he said.

"This is Andrew Taylor. I've spoken to Police Chief Dexter. He'll arrive at the hotel at eight-thirty to talk with you and Mrs. Cerone about the stakeout. He's bringing two officers with him."

"Thanks, Mr. Taylor," Frank said, before he hung up the phone. "It's all set," he told his father and Joe. "The police will get here before nine. So, what should we do while we wait for the police to show up?"

Joe moved over to the night table and picked up the phone. "There's something I forgot to tell Mike Strauss. He's got to send us up some breakfast before I starve!"

At eight-thirty the phone rang, and Frank picked it up. "That was Strauss," Frank told Joe and their father. "The police just got here. They're heading over to a conference room off the lobby. Strauss saw Mrs. Cerone go into the room a few minutes ago. We'd better get down there."

The three Hardys left the room and took the elevator down to the lobby. When they got off the elevator, Frank led them over to a room opposite the phone booths. He opened the door and stepped inside, followed by Joe and Fenton.

Inside the room stood a burly, balding police officer who looked to be in his fifties. With him were two younger officers. The burly officer was talking to a short, gray-haired woman sitting in one of the chairs at the conference table.

"I'm Fenton Hardy and these are my sons, Frank and Joe," Fenton said to the officers.

"I'm Police Chief Alan Dexter," the burly officer said gruffly. "I was just explaining to Mrs. Cerone here that she's been the victim of a scam and that we need her to help us catch the scam artists."

"They seemed so genuine," Mrs. Cerone said with a sigh. "It's hard to believe they're nothing but con artists." She looked up at Chief Dexter, a fearful expression on her face. "Will I be in any danger?" she asked nervously.

"We'll be in the conference room next door watching every move the scam artists make," Chief Dexter said reassuringly. "We won't let anything happen to you."

The chief looked at his watch. "We'd better begin our stakeout." He looked at Fenton Hardy. "You and your sons can join the stakeout if you want. Just don't get in our way."

"We won't," Fenton assured him.

The officers and the Hardys filed into the conference room next door. Chief Dexter opened the connecting door just wide enough to see into the next room. His officers stood behind him.

"What's taking them so long?" Joe muttered after fifteen minutes had passed. "They should have been here by now."

Just then, he heard a man's cheerful voice say, "Here we are, Mrs. Cerone. Are you ready to buy yourself a beautiful new condo?"

"Oh, yes," Mrs. Cerone replied. "I've got the check right here."

"You can give that to me," another female voice said.

Frank and Joe waited tensely. They saw Chief Dexter quietly slip the gun from his holster. Then he jerked open the door, and he and his officers rushed into the conference room. "Police. Freeze!" the chief shouted.

The Hardys followed them into the room in time to see a red-haired man's hand move toward his jacket pocket. Joe sprang forward and grabbed his wrist. "Oh, no, you don't," he said, removing the gun from the man's pocket.

"Well, if it isn't Steve Willis," Frank said. He raised the man's wrist and saw the red watch with the black, star-shaped dial. Then he pulled off the man's red wig, revealing a dark crewcut underneath.

"So you caught me," Willis snarled, as Chief Dexter clapped handcuffs on his wrists. "I should

136

have pushed you off that roller coaster when I had the chance."

Meanwhile, Joe approached the young woman. "Don't bother," she snapped, pulling off her blond wig to reveal short brown hair. "I'm Laurel Kramer."

"Take them down to the station," Chief Dexter said to the two police officers.

After the officers ushered Kramer and Willis out the door, Chief Dexter turned to Mrs. Cerone.

"You did a great job, ma'am," he said.

"I was terrified the entire time," she admitted with a shaky smile. "But this will be a good story to tell my grandchildren."

After she had left the room with an officer, Frank turned to Chief Dexter. "Are you going to arrest Justin Maceda now?" he asked the chief. "Andrew Taylor should know where he is."

Chief Dexter shook his head. "Taylor asked me the same question," he replied. "You'll have to get a confession from Maceda in order to prove his involvement in the scam operation and Mr. Hardy's kidnapping. Right now, we have nothing against him except your word that he's involved."

"What can we do?" Joe asked.

"Well, you could confront him with one of you wearing a wire," Chief Dexter said. "But that could be dangerous."

"We'll risk it," Frank said. "I'll wear the wire."

"I've got the equipment in my car," the chief said. "I'll bring it up to your room."

Fifteen minutes later, Frank was carefully putting his T-shirt back on over wires and tiny microphones taped to his chest.

"Everything you and Maceda say will be transmitted here and taped," Chief Dexter said, patting a small black box he had placed on the desk.

At that moment, the phone began to ring, and Joe picked it up.

"Something terrible has happened," Andrew Taylor said in an agitated voice. "Justin Maceda has escaped!"

15 Escape to a New Dimension

"What do you mean Maceda escaped?" Joe asked Taylor. "Tell me exactly what happened."

"I sent for Maceda, who was in his workroom at the Hall of Holograms," Taylor told him. "We discussed the new Space Needle in my office for a while. Then I had breakfast brought in. At around ten o'clock, one of Chief Dexter's officers phoned to tell me she had apprehended Laurel Kramer and Steve Willis. I had swiveled around in my chair and my back was to Maceda."

There was a pause at the other end of the line.

"Well?" Joe demanded. "What happened next?"

"Without thinking, I said, 'I'm glad you caught Kramer and Willis, Officer,'" Taylor admitted.

"When I turned to face Maceda he was gone. He wasn't in his office, and no one saw him leave the building. I've had security guards posted at all the exits to the park."

"Good thinking," Joe said. He hung up the phone and told the others what had happened.

"He must have used the bookcase in his office to enter the underground area," Frank said. "If he's still down there, we'll find him."

"Security will stop him if he tries to leave the park," Chief Dexter said. "The trouble is, I can't legally hold him for long without real proof that he's done something wrong."

"We'll get proof," Joe declared.

"Maceda's pretty clever," Frank pointed out. "Even if we do get him to confess, he might figure out a way to escape afterward. Wait a minute," Frank said suddenly. "Why don't we use one of our ID badges to track him like he tracked us?" He turned to his father. "Did you bring a modem with your laptop computer?"

"Yes, but what are you getting at, Frank?" Fenton asked.

"I'm thinking that maybe Maceda is on the National Network—the network that links computers in universities and libraries," Frank replied. "Your computer at home is on the NatNet, too. If you use the laptop and modem to tap into your PC, maybe you can hack your way into Maceda's computer and access the program he used to track us."

"It's worth a try," Fenton said as Joe handed him the computer. "I'll work as quickly as I can, but it may take me a while to come up with Maceda's password, assuming I can manage to figure it out at all. In any case, you guys had better get going."

"We're on our way," Joe said. He grabbed his badge and flashlight off the desk. Then he and his brother hurried out the door.

"Where do you think Maceda is?" Frank asked as they exited the hotel.

"If I were him, I'd be in that room under the Home of the Future trying to destroy any evidence of the scam operation," Joe replied.

"Makes sense," Frank said. He looked up at the monorail. "I think we can get there faster on foot than by train."

As they walked quickly toward the Home of the Future, Joe suddenly began to feel tired. The lack of sleep was finally catching up to him. But he shook off his exhaustion and picked up his pace. First he and Frank had to collar Maceda. Then they could sleep.

When the brothers reached the Home of the Future, they saw a sign on the door that read Exhibit Closed. Inside, a maintenance crew was cleaning up the mess from the night before. The floors were still wet from the washing machine overflow, and the fire extinguisher foam had hardened on the furniture and walls.

"You wouldn't happen to know how this happened?" one of the maintenance workers asked Joe, who was still wearing his staff uniform.

"I don't have a clue," Joe said casually. "But Mr. Taylor sent us over to see how the cleanup was going. My brother is on the staff, too, but his uniform is being cleaned."

The worker nodded, then continued mopping the floor.

Frank and Joe headed over to the closet. Making sure the cleaning man couldn't see them, they stepped inside and opened the door leading to the underground area. They could see that the overhead light was on in the room below.

Frank closed the secret door behind them, then he and Joe crept down the steps. They were almost at the bottom when they spotted Justin Maceda in a corner, feeding papers into a shredder. Slowly and quietly, they moved toward him. As they got closer, Frank saw a briefcase sitting on the floor beside him.

Maceda sensed the Hardys' presence and turned to face them, a black laser gun in his hand. "I had a feeling you would find me," Maceda snarled.

"It's too bad you'll have to cancel your plans for that theme park," Frank said quietly.

"You kid detectives have ruined everything," Maceda cried. "I could have opened a special high-tech park designed and owned by *me*, not that money-grubbing Andrew Taylor. My park would have featured robots and the most advanced video games and holography ever designed. I've dreamed of my own park for years."

"But you needed money to fulfill that dream," Frank prompted.

"Of course," Maceda snapped. "Why do you think I started my little scam operation and recruited Laurel Kramer and Steve Willis to pose as developers? I planned to pay them part of the profits from my park."

"Did you also have them kidnap our father?" Joe asked.

"He was getting too nosy," Maceda said, scowling. He jerked his head toward the secret door. "I spotted him snooping around in the closet up there, and knew he had to be stopped. I got Mike Strauss to give me his name and tell me where he was from. The librarian at Bayport Public Library was quite talkative, too. She was happy to tell me all about Fenton Hardy, the famous private investigator, and his two detective sons."

"You were going to stop Dad—by killing him," Joe said in an accusing tone.

"Yes, well, I like to cover all the bases," Maceda replied. "He knew the details of the scam operation. And even though Laurel and Steve were always disguised when they visited your father, he just might have noticed something about them, or they might have said something that revealed their identities. And I couldn't take the chance that, if they were caught, they would implicate me."

143

He glared at the Hardys. "But I didn't figure on you two. I told you your father was investigating my stolen blueprints to keep you off my trail. I was convinced you would give up the investigation after I had Willis call and warn you to leave the Fourth Dimension. But I was wrong."

"So you planted homing devices in our ID badges and tracked us with your computer," Frank said.

"Very good. I did it to keep you from exploring the underground area. It's always been the perfect hiding place. No one ever comes here without my authorization, and Andrew thinks it's merely a storage area for my failed experiments."

Maceda shrugged. "I tried to stop you by putting obstacles in your path," he continued. "The out-of-control virtual reality game, Space Shuttle Simulator, and Home of the Future were all programmed from my computer. I was determined to make you give up the search. Then I left that note under your door. But I was sure you'd completely lose hope of ever finding your father when you saw that hologram I prepared of him."

"Did Steve Willis cause that virtual reality game to malfunction?" Frank asked. "And was he driving the hovercraft car that tried to deck Ernest Brody?"

"Yes to both questions," Maceda said, a sly smile on his face. "Steve spotted that old fool Brody when the three of you were having lunch. He recognized Brody as one of his scam victims. And he wasn't happy to see him talking."

"Anyway, we didn't give up," Joe said. "Not even

144

that phone call from Willis—when he told us to leave the park—could stop us."

"No," Maceda said flatly. "Not even when I had your father moved to the clock tower. Willis did that after you and Brody entered the Home of the Future."

He picked up a pair of goggles off the table and put them on. "I'm afraid I can't stay here and chat with you any longer," he said, raising his laser gun. "My hovercraft is waiting for me. By the time you tell the authorities what I've just revealed to you, I'll be far away in another state, with a new identity.

"This laser gun is similar to the one Laurel used on you in the arena, Frank," Maceda continued. "But it has another special feature, which can only be used once. I'll show you."

He adjusted the gun and pointed it at the overhead lamp. While Maceda's eyes were on the lamp, Joe quickly pulled the ID badge out of his pocket and tossed it into Maceda's briefcase.

At that moment, Maceda fired. The bulb exploded, and then a bright white light filled the room. Frank and Joe instinctively covered their eyes.

Then the light faded, leaving the Hardys in total darkness. Suddenly, they heard the sound of footsteps running through the underground area.

"He's heading north," Joe said, switching on his flashlight. "Come on!"

As they raced after Maceda, they heard the sound of his footsteps grow fainter, then stop.

The Hardys continued on. When they reached the Hall of Holograms, Joe shined the flashlight up on the steps and saw that the door was open.

Joe and Frank rushed up the steps, with Joe leading the way. A few feet inside the room, Joe stopped short. "I don't believe what I'm seeing," he whispered.

Ahead of them, spaced throughout the room, were four Justin Macedas glowing in the light of laser beams.

Frank and Joe darted behind a packing case near the door and crouched down. The images stood silent and unmoving before them.

"Which is the real Maceda?" Frank whispered as he peered over the top of the case. "Or are they all holograms? This could be another one of his tricks."

"They're kind of blurry," Joe murmured. "I can't tell if Maceda still has his gun."

Suddenly he noticed a Maceda that was standing half in and half out of one of the laser lights. Joe raised his flashlight and shined it directly on the side of the face that was in the shadows. The figure blinked and turned its head away from Joe's light.

With a cry of anger, Maceda rushed forward, his laser gun aimed right at Joe's head!

16 War of the Worlds

Joe dropped down behind a crate. A split second later, he heard a hissing sound from the burning hole the laser beam had made in the wall behind him.

Frank sprang out from behind the crate and hurled himself at Maceda. The architect immediately pointed his gun at him. Frank dove to the floor and rolled away just as Maceda pulled the trigger.

Suddenly, the door leading to the exhibit burst open and Fenton Hardy rushed into the room, followed by Police Chief Dexter. Before Maceda could react, Fenton grabbed him and squeezed his wrist tightly. The gun fell out of Maceda's hand and clattered to the floor.

147

Chief Dexter found the light switch and flicked it on. Fenton turned Maceda over to him, then reached down to help Frank off the floor.

"What took *you* so long?" Frank said with a grin as he got to his feet.

Fenton laughed. "I guess I deserve that," he said, smiling at his son. "Actually, it took me a while to access your file in Maceda's computer."

"You think you're so clever, using my own homing device to track me," Maceda burst out. "But you can't prove I committed any crime except firing a laser gun."

"That alone should put you away for a while," Frank said. "But we can also prove that you ran a scam operation and arranged a kidnapping." He turned to Chief Dexter. "Right?"

He smiled and nodded. "The wire worked perfectly. We got Maceda's entire confession on tape. And now I'd better get him into police custody," he added, taking Maceda's arm.

"Thanks for all your help, Chief Dexter," Joe said, as the police chief escorted Maceda out the door.

"Let's get rid of these guys," Frank said, motioning toward the three holograms of Justin Maceda. He located the laser boxes and switched them off. The holograms faded from sight.

"There's one thing that puzzles me," Fenton said. "Why did Maceda stop in here and activate the holograms? Why didn't he just run out of the building?"

"My guess is he came in here to get this," Joe said, stepping over to Maceda's open briefcase, which was sitting on the floor in front of a worktable. He reached down and picked up a blueprint. "Just what I suspected. This is the design for a holograph exhibit at his theme park. Maceda activated the holograms to confuse us in case we got up here before he had a chance to escape. I guess he didn't cover his bases very well," Joe continued, yawning.

Frank yawned, too. Then he grinned. "If Aunt Gertrude were here, do you think she'd tell us that nothing is more important for teenagers than a good night's sleep?"

Joe laughed. "I hate to admit it, but this is one time I totally agree with her!"

Late the next morning, Frank, Joe, Fenton, and Brody sat in the Galaxy's restaurant having breakfast.

"There are still a couple of missing pieces to the puzzle," Joe said to his father. "Did you drop your watch hoping we'd find it and figure out where you were?"

Fenton put down his coffee cup and nodded. "At one point, Kramer and Willis came down to the underground room together. They gave me food, then regagged me and took a photo of me. That must have been the photo Maceda used in the hologram you told me about.

"I overheard them say that if anything went

wrong, they would take me to the clock tower," he continued. "Since I knew you'd find your way down there, I decided to try and leave my watch as a clue, just in case they did move me. It took a while, but I managed to undo the clasp and work the watch around the ropes."

"Why did you hide the map with the circled buildings on it in your glasses case?" Frank asked.

"First I circled the buildings to remind me which ones contained the secret entrances," Fenton explained. "Then I hid the map in case my room was searched. A detective can't be too careful. Of course," he added with a sigh, "if I'd been *really* careful, I probably wouldn't have gotten myself kidnapped in the first place."

"Don't blame yourself," Ernest Brody said. "Those kidnappers were pretty sneaky. In fact, if it hadn't been for Frank and Joe, I would have been sharing that underground room with you."

Just then, Chief Dexter approached them. "I wanted you to know that Laurel Kramer and Steve Willis gave us full confessions last night. Willis said that he chloroformed Mike Strauss and robbed the safe. He knocked out Strauss so that he and Kramer could get Mr. Hardy out of the hotel without being seen. The theft was committed to make the crime look like a robbery.

"They drove Mr. Hardy over to the Biosphere in a maintenance cart," Chief Dexter continued. "They were dressed as maintenance workers and had a story ready in case security stopped them. After they tied Mr. Hardy up, Willis returned to the hotel and put back the master key."

"Did Willis say that he was Mr. Brody's would-be kidnapper dressed as an alien?" Joe asked. "And was Willis the guy who was dressed as a maintenance worker who rigged that model of earth to fall?"

Chief Dexter nodded. "Yes, he did both of those things."

"Whose idea was it for Laurel to pose as a chambermaid?" Frank wanted to know.

"Maceda's," Chief Dexter replied. "He knew they'd have to get rid of Mr. Hardy's things." He smiled at Frank and Joe. "Any other questions?"

Both Hardys stood up. "I think that about wraps it up," Frank said.

A few minutes after Chief Dexter had left, the Hardys saw a young man and woman coming toward them dressed in dark blue pants and shiny gold shirts with dark blue lightning stripes down the front and back.

"We're asking some of the guests if they'd like to take part in a War of the Worlds laser gun game today," the young man said. He looked at Frank and Joe. "Would you guys be interested?"

The brothers looked at each other and laughed. Then Frank turned to the two staffers and said, "Thanks, but no thanks. I think we've fought our war already."

"And won it," Joe added, giving his brother a high-five.